Michael Levy

Cutting Truths

Fifty Enlightening Slices of Life

Website: http://www.pointoflife.com

ISBN: 0981936717
ISBN-13: 9780981936710
Library of Congress Control Number: 2010909196

SLICE ONE
Freedom of Thought

Myths and legends give birth to enchanting hues and flavors in a human race with vivid imaginations. Some say modern day religion derives its themes from mythology. Any student can detect many similarities in religion that could have foundation in earlier folklore. For instance, there are numerous virgin births in mythology well before the story of Jesus came on the human stage.

Modern religion relates to one male God who rules the heavens and earth. Perhaps that is why a Shakespeare character once remarked ... "Being born is like being sold into slavery."

A child's impression of God is a man in a white robe and long beard that will punish them unless they follow their holy books instructions. Likewise, many children imagine a unicorn to be a horse with a horn on its head that has mystical powers. Both images are real to the holder of the thoughts.

When children mature, most realize the unicorn is just a flight of fantasy. However, the majority will continue with their be-lie-f in a male God that can strike anger and revenge at his human subjects, if they do not worship and obey him.

Indoctrinated fear builds this male god into a monster that can kill babies with death angels and can bring plagues of many varieties to a people who lose be-lie-f in this human type of trendsetter.

It seems the more fundamental the followers become of a male macho God, the more the risk of wars and terrorist attacks. Faithful followers of their male, image-maker have slaughtered millions. No doubt, many more will perish in the name of holy wars directed by their personal, one true God, who will bring his faithful people to a glorious victory in heaven and send the rest to damnation in hell. It would make super fiction stories, unfortunately, the history of religious wars are a major blot on the human landscape and still exist today.

The authentic side of all religions is the spiritual essence that flows through them. This is the good facet of a universal creator/evolver and is no different from the spirit that nurtured many ancient tribes. They were nurtured on folk law tales of wizards and witches, dragons and knights, evil and good spirits in all kind of guises. Indeed, even today, there are sections of humanity that use different symbols and customs than that of modern day religion, For instance, sweat lodges and rites of nature, still furnish spiritual devotion for people thirsty for a sound conviction base.

In ancient Egyptian, Persian, Roman and Greek times, the gods and goddesses played many tricks on the human race. Only the bravest and purest humans could make their journey to heavenly immortality, whilst all the less deserving were sent down into the fires of Hades ... hell to you and I. ... Yes, the ingenuity of heaven and hell has been around for thousands of years. Well before the monolithic God was established as the momentous super-intendent.

The female in all species on earth give birth, not the male. Subsequently, perhaps if we go back far enough, we may find out if the same goddesses that prevailed over the heaven and earth countless years ago still exist in this era.

For a few moments, let us visualize a world directed by the Sea Goddess...

What a wonderful image it creates when we go down to the beach to bathe in the clear waters of the Sea Goddess. She welcomes us into her open arms with sensual, curvaceous pleasure. The warm water feels as though we are back in the womb and verily we are.

We enter into the ebbing womb of the sea goddess. We feel her loving textures as the water laps its caresses over timeworn bodies. We are children of earth, running into nature's oceanic tides and time. All the oceans wrapped around the supporting arms of the sea goddess as we bathe in gladness.

The Greeks named Tethys and Thetis, as the great Mistress of the Sea. However, the Sea Goddess was recognizable in many forms and names, by legions of ancient dynasties. One could claim she is the mother of all earth, for everyone needs water to survive and grow. Religion declares humans are built in the image of God. Moreover, since our bodies are eighty percent water, a part of the sea goddess could profess to be inside us all.

Maybe we can start a fresh, modern day myth, which brings satisfying delights and enchantment to people who need something to support their daily toil. Who knows, it may even establish a future religion?

When the waters break inside the womb, a woman opens her legs to allow her child to come into the world. As it enters the world, the loving sea goddess, with open arms and a joyful, angelic smile, embraces it. Her intent is for every baby that comes into the world to understand it will always have loving, joy-filled arms to embrace them, every moment on earth... Just as long as their image of whom they truly are, (a spiritual child of the universe) does not ever forsake them.

No matter whom you believe your God to be, as long as you live with the spirit of the universe within your conscious mind, you can be, whatever you wish to be. You can visualize, whatever you wish to imagine. In every mystical experience, whatever you imagine, that is where you are at that moment in time. The metaphysical world of the sea goddess is one of the multi-layered realms of great mystics.

Mysticism is the ability to use cosmic, x-ray visions, to peer though the shams and masquerades the ego boasts as its factualness. Performing to the best of ones ability on the stage of earth can be a great joy, once a person comprehends there is always someone with loving arms and smiling face, to catch them, when they fall from grace... To transport them to peaceful, gently flowing, calming, still waters. The sea goddess is there for all who believe.

In all form and gender ...God is God ... God is Good.

To have hope there needs to be belief, to hold belief there needs to be doubt, to have no doubt of the truth there is no need for hope or belief.

SLICE TWO
Lessons in The World of Myths.

Here are a few examples, from a multitude of Greek stories, that all have a moral lesson and conceivably metaphysical, spiritual meaning behind them...

Phaethon.
Phaethon, a mortal who was said to be the son of the Sun, borrowed the chariot of the Sun for a day. His father begged him not to take the chariot for it was even difficult for him to drive it. But as many sons do, Phaethon ignored the advice and disobeyed the instructions on how to drive. He drove far too near the earth and set it alight. He lost control of the Suns chariot and the only way to stop his wild ride was for Zeus to strike him dead with a thunderbolt. He fell into a river, where his sisters mourned for him until they were both turned into poplar trees, their tears changed into drops of amber, which seeped from the trees.

Lesson.
How many children have burnt their hands in the fire to see if it was hot, even when their parents said not to do it? Honor thy mother and father, would be a fitting moral to this story. However, maybe there is a lot more to this story....

The modern media sends messages all around the world scorching the earth with negativity, sensationalism and unsavory news. It digs deep to find all the losers of humanity and then fires off its opinions to all who have been brainwashed into being addicted to negative news and unsavory programs on TV. Yes, the media is like a naughty child chasing around the globe setting fire to peace and contentment, serenity and tranquility. Is there a thunderbolt of intelligence ready to strike at their close-minded attitude to authentic meaning?

Can the pollution that is belching out around the world because of ignorant corporation policies be stopped by people with deep-felt love of mother earth?

Will the depletion of fish from our over fished oceans stop?

Will the depletion of trees in the rain forest stop?

Will humanities unconstrained ride of insane wars, scorching earth with bombs, come to an end any time soon?

Will crime and poverty be extinguished from our city streets?

Will our civilization take notice of universal intelligence that controls nature?

Well, even if we cannot stop humanities wild ride of ignorance, at the end of the story tears of sorrow turned to amber, which is today worn as jewelry. This can signify the fact that although a person dies in physical form, some part of them remains on earth in many differing guises. A type of reincarnation perhaps, turning sorrow into a bright, colorful substance that gives joy to folks?

Persephone.

Demeter was the sister of Zeus and the mother of beautiful Persephone. One day Persephone was gathering wild flowers in the meadow when a huge crack opened up in the earth. Hades god of the dead emerged from the underworld. He seized Persephone and carried her off in his carriage, back down to the underworld. Hades forced her to marry him and he made her queen of the underworld. Demeter, who was goddess of agriculture, wandered the length and the breath of earth in search of her daughter. Whilst her attention was taken away from her job protecting the crops they withered up and died from the cold weather.

Lesson.

Many events happen to us in our lifetime. We are all given a mission of creativity to perform on earth. They say life is what happens to us whilst we make plans. Many times our focus and true intent is overcome by events we have no control over. If we allow our lives to be ruled by devastations and uncertainty, we will become wandering nomads that can find no authentic meaning of life. Our lives on earth are limited in a short time framework.

Nobody knows what tomorrow may bring, so with this in mind perhaps we should always make the most of all the good and bad that befalls our three dimensional existence. If we are dislodged from our source, our true intent may become tainted with the illusions of unreliable concepts, questionable perceptions and misguided thoughts.

Heracles.

Heracles was the son of Zeus and Hera. He was the Greeks biggest hero performing twelve labors after killing his own children because his mother drove him mad. (Any lessons to learn here). Many of the labors involved killing monsters and saving earth from dangers. One of the labors required Heracles to hold up one of the pillars, which held up the heavens. He did this for a while and then gave the task back to Atlas. In most of his quests ingenuity and inventiveness was more essential then his great strength He ended up as a god in the heavens for his good deeds on earth. Sampson's feats of strength fade into cloudiness when compared to those of Heracles, however both were heroes of their society.

Lesson.

When we follow the path universal intelligence has laid out for humanity, we succeed in all our endeavors because we used our inherent wisdom and intuitive ingenuity to overcome and solve any adversity that came our way. Often, not brute strength solves our problems, but an awareness of danger and the common sense to deal with it. When force is required, it is used with good intent, to protect and defend the innocent.

Jason and the Quest for the Golden Fleece.

Jason was another great, likable hero. An unlawful king would have killed Jason at birth but for his mother hiding him in a cave (Moses was hidden in bulrushes) When he was a youth he performed a good deed helping an old woman across a raging river. The old withered woman was none other than Hera wife of Zeus. He was well protected for giving his unconditional help.

His task to obtain the Golden Fleece is filled with many exciting adventures and the killing of dragons and monsters. He not only uses his strength, but more than that, uses wisdom and skill in overcoming many adversities sent to test his metal. His first encounter was with a band of beautiful women and it was here he had his first sexual experience. He later listened to advice in fighting his foes from an enchantress, who fell in love with him, which showed his ability to take advice from others. All his tasks were a true test of Greek manhood and like Heracles his brain was mightier that his brawn.

Lesson.

In today's world, the Jewish religion only requires the youth to recite a portion of the torah to become a man. It is a tradition that has been enacted over the past eight hundred years, so it is relatively new in religious terms.

In the legend of King Arthur brave knights would go on quests to show their honor and manliness. The San-greal or as most know it, the Holy Grail... Old English for Grail, thought to be the cup of Jesus at the last supper, was a quest in search of a symbol of Christianity. This then clearly connects legend and religion. Many other myths can be associated with stories in the bible.

The Greeks had a great flood that destroyed all the wicked people except for an old man and his wife who went up the mountain for protection. Noah built an ark.

In another myth somebody was turned to stone for looking back, disobeying instructions, in the same way as Lots wife.

The foundations of many biblical tales are found in many Greek myths. Which begs the question where do myths and legends stop and real facts project authenticity? I guess the answer is blowing in the wind, so perhaps we should ask the wind god?

Theseus.

Theseus was one of the Greek heroes whose father was a king. He retrieved a magical sword from under a heavy rock using strength skill and leverage (Did any English knight of the round table do a similar act a few thousand years later) He traveled great distances fighting many scoundrels and killed them in the same manner they were tormenting and killing other folks. (Karma) One of his main encounters was with the feared Minotaur (half bull and half man) who lived in a maze called the labyrinth that imprisoned him. Theseus was aided by a woman, who fell in love with him and she gave him a ball of thread that he attached to the opening of the maze, so that he could find his way out. He killed the Minotaur with his magic sword and went back to Athens where he becomes the king. He was the guy who took Helen from Troy. He ruled in a fair manner and was renowned for his justice, wisdom and kindness. Some say this story is historical rather than mythical.

Perhaps Theseus was the Greeks version of tale of Solomon? A wise, strong king who loved a non- Hebrew named Sheba..... Many of these tales show the importance of wisdom.

Lesson.

How many schools and universities focus their attention on teaching wisdom to their students today? More to the point, how many teachers have the wisdom to teach others?

Inner wisdom is the greatest gift all mortals possess. Many seek their wisdom all their lives and the search becomes a fool's errand... For all the time they were seeking, it was buried deep inside them and that was the only place they did not think to look. Just like the ripples in a pond, whatever we think about and perform...we will make reflective waves that may have dire consequences if inner wisdom was ignored and our ego was our only guide.

Narcissus and Echo.

Echo was a beautiful nymph, But Echo had one failing, and she was too fond of talking and would always have the last word. She upset the goddess Hera and thus forfeited the use of her tongue, except for the fact she could have the last word, but no power to speak first.

One day Echo saw Narcissus, a beautiful youth. She fell in love with him and followed his footsteps wherever he went. She tried to attract his attention but failed. Her love was too strong for the one person, who only loved himself. She pined away and it was in a cave where all her flesh shrank away into nothingness. Her bones transformed into rocks and there was nothing left of her but her voice. Even today, an echo always has the last word.

Narcissus eluded all the other nymphs, as he had the pitiful Echo. One day he stooped down to drink at a pool, and saw his own image in the water; he thought it such a beautiful sight to behold. He stood gazing with admiration at his own beauty and fell deeply in love with himself. Alas, he could not touch himself. Eventually, infatuated so much for himself, he withered away and died. The nymphs could not find his body, so they planted a purple flower surrounded with white leaves which preserved the memory of Narcissus.

Lesson.

How many people live a superficial, shallow life, only interested in preserving their possessions and good looks at the expense of their inner serenity and tranquility?

How many people die of disease caused by worry and anxiety, pining for things outside their reach?

How many people live with regrets and woes, languishing in regret for things that slipped through their fingers?

So close and yet so far away, just as the water slipped through the fingers of Narcissus Conceivably, the greatest Greek philosopher was Plato. One of the passages he wrote was about a man who was imprisoned with chains attached to his head. He could only look forward and when he heard voices coming from the side and rear he could only see the voices coming out of shadows. He lived most of his life believing that shadows could speak. Then one day, when he was old and grey, he was released from his shackles and could slowly turn around and see the reality of who was speaking. The illusions of the shadows speaking were for the first time revealed for what they were. Just shadows of the real thing. How many beliefs in today's world are just shadows speaking?

In all the stories, in all the religions, there lives one ongoing theme... The immortal soul of humanity. It is nourished by a godly spirit, so there can be no denying the existence in the minds of all believers, in the mysterious omnipresence of a supreme power that has control of all things bright and beautiful.

Perhaps all the negative stuff comes from the free will of mortals, who can turn paradise on earth into a hellish inferno of ignorance? Many religions preach hell and damnation if we do not follow their way of thinking. Since it was probably the Greeks who invented hell in an intellectual sense, I wonder why there is no reference to the ancient myths in any bible. Could humanity be ready for an authentic archeological dig?

Although most of the heroes of Greek mythology did great heroic deeds, most of them had egotistical weaknesses such as pride, envy, gluttony, lust, anger, greed and sloth, but so did their gods.

Which begs the question, are all the ancient gods, man-made projections of the egotistical, dualistic system of human thinking? For sure, the modern religious God has many dualistic unfavorable qualities that emanate from man made negative emotions. Are we then trapped in an every spinning web of misinformation within the realms of creation/evolving from an omnipresent super power?

I guess if we can only view God in human terms, we are doomed to live a life of dualistic good and evil. However, if we can look beyond intellectual understanding and see humanity in a clearer way...as a light, in a universal lamp. Then perhaps we can illuminate our existence on earth and shy away from the myths and legends in our religions.

If we can leave out all the hell, damnation, revenge and anger that were born in classical tales of fantasy, we may be able to restructure world religions into the spiritual guidance it is meant to be. By omitting the entire unnecessary dogmatic ingredient in religious soup, humanity will be able to focus on the mysterious wonderment of creation/evolving. A projection that allows all creatures large and small to live a life filled with love & joy, with no requirement to question why universal intelligence controls the universe.

To put it another way ... To live a perfect life in the afterlife, it seems we need to live an authentic life in our physical life here on earth. If there is no after life, then it is even more essential to live an authentic life, without negative stressful emotions, emitted from the minds illusionary myths. Now after all that, how about a nice refreshing dish of ambrosia, washed down with a cool glass of nectar.

A billion inspirational dreams are deposited in the Unicorn bank of wishful thinking ...
Do you know you hold the key to realize them?

SLICE THREE
A Tale of Karma

Once upon a time ago in a big country, two bright boys grew up in a small town. Tom and Dick were twelve years old and both were top of the same class. Tom had the brains; Dick was good at tricky scheming and cribbing. Tom was lean and wiry, Dick was fat and greedy. Dick came from a rich family and had plenty of spending money, whilst Tom came from a humble back ground and earned his spending money doing a newspaper round in the early mornings and washing cars at the weekends.

One day Dick told Tom he had just made up a new game, he would go into the candy store which was run by an old man who was in his late seventy's, slightly deaf and with bad eyesight. Dick would wait for the old man to be distracted for a moment and steal his favorite candy bar which was stacked on the front counter. Tom tried to persuade Dick to stop his game but Dick thought it was good fun to rob the old man and laughed at Tom's request.

Dick said he would play this game four times a week in the mornings before he went to school. The Newspaper store where Tom worked was next door to another candy store. Tom decided he would buy the same candy from this store and place the candy on the old mans counter the same days Dick would steal one.

Tom was not a snitch and although he had little money he would right the wrong.

As luck would have it a few months went by and Dick's father got a new job in a different part of the country so they had to move. Although Tom and Dick were friends Tom was relieved to see the back of Dick.

Their paths would not cross for many years. They were now both in their fiftieth year and very successful in their own Hi-tech businesses. Tom had found his success by going down the correct path but Dick had used espionage and cheating to crawl his way to success.

They both met one day at a convention and greeted each other fondly. They both ran similar businesses and were keen to catch up with the past. They went out for a meal together and Tom told Dick he was on the threshold of the most amazing discovery of all time. Some software that would better the lives of everybody on the Planet; it would also make Tom a multi-billionaire. Tom said it would be a month before the final conclusions were made but he was positive it was a winner. Now Dick was an expert at espionage and that night Dick phoned his henchmen to break into Tom's building and without anyone knowing to steal the new plans.

This he did and within a fortnight had the model up and running. It was a simple discovery but no one had thought of it before.

Both companies announced the new discovery at the same time and of course, a large law suit followed.

Tom Angel verses Dick Deville, presiding judge Harry Karma Jnr. Tom knew he had seen the judge somewhere before but he could not remember where.

Both parties agreed to abide by the judges decision. Dick thought he could hoodwink the judge just as had hoodwinked everyone all his life.

Wise judge Harry said he will ask one question. He turned to Dick and asked "How did you discover this amazing finding?"

I have A University degree in technology. I have studied many academic books and analytical theories. After many years of study realized I was far more intellectually brilliant than anyone else in my field. The discovery came to my superior analytical brain from study. I have an intellect that is far superior to Tom Angel so you see your honor; it must have been me who invented this software.

He then turned to Tom. "Tell me how you made the discovery?"

I too have studied many books and theories, however I realized something was missing. I wanted to understand where all intelligence came from. What was the source of intelligent energy which is part humankind's construction and fiber? Many years of deep thought and inner questioning allowed my mind to decode the signals that the Universe holds. My subconscious mind continually asked the same question over and over. Through a series of silent meditations after many years, I finally decoded the messages correctly and the discovery was made.

Judge Karma stood up and said there is no doubt whatsoever that Mr. Tom Angel is the man who made the discovery. Mr. Deville has committed a criminal act and now a civil action will have to be turned into criminal case.

It took a while for Tom to remember where we had seen the judge before. Then it dawned on him the judge was the son of Harry Senior that ran the candy store in his home town. But how could that be the store keeper was nearly eighty and the judge the same age.

The store keeper and the judge were natural human wizards of Karmic actions. There are many wizards located all over the world in differing guises. Human wizards constantly perform life's innovative miracles and the laws of Karma keep the world in perfect balance.

In conclusion: Tom Angel opened many authentic learning and understanding centers titled, Love, Harmony and Joy Centers. Now all human beings throughout the world can tune into Toms Love Harmony and Joy.

When Dick Deville reached his eightieth birthday he was released from jail, a frail withering old man with no money and nowhere to go. Located near the prison was a Love Harmony and Joy center. Dick walked across the road and fell on his knees and kissed the steps of the building.

The Moral
Love Harmony and Joy will bring the Devil (Deville) to his knees

When we release the necessity to be right, we can obtain the wisdom to live in peaceful tranquility.

SLICE FOUR
Self Delusions of Mr. & Mrs. Humbug

Throughout all our yesteryears, mankind has erroneously manufactured a counterfeit image of itself. This identity currently projects itself on a screen of reality, now playing in a narrow minded neighborhood somewhere near you. Many characters make up this act and the leading roles are given to those who can fit into the "normal" bogus roles the best. It seems in most instances the higher the education, the more distant the insights into higher realities or dare we say "Authentic Divine Guidance"

The most important roles are given to the willing actors, whose well rehearsed script is precisely memorized, then spoken. All is neatly produced by scholars from the School of Egotism. These folks control many parts of our societies "normal" today. The one thing most of them lack is wisdom but no matter, let the masquerade emerge from its self acclaiming academics, media and all other singular truth organizations. Pats on the back are the order of the day for the alien members of egos fluff-stuff. Enter the human academy of singular truth science, politics, media, finance and religion.

Mr. & Mrs. Humbug are great supporters of the Academy of Egotism. They 'I'_dolize it. Their roles take place in the back lots of life's studios. It all seems so real but behind the frail frames of the facade, many horrific scenes take place.

Many folks with high intellect seem to believe modern science is a method by which we can detach ourselves from nature and become aloof from a higher reality. Whilst science brings us many new discoveries, many intellects say everything happens "by chance" and there is no meaning to life other than "real facts in science" They become their own devil-gods and believe they have full power over their domain. Their reasoning guides them to judge life in terms of intellectual reasoning and logic, to be cultivated by mathematical proof. If they can't prove it, well it just does not exist.

Mr. & Mrs. Humbug Live at No 1 Ignorance Blvd., Mayhem Town, Disbelief-in-the Truth City, US-Less

Human beings who walk alone thinking they are somehow detached from the universe, act as chaotic particles of energy. Many will say they are merely the chemical reactions of the brain. For folks who talk in this manner, well, that is all they are at that moment...A mass of chemical reactions, with intellects/egos that contain very little authentic meaning.

Mr. and Mrs. Humbug like to picnic by ingesting "Media Porky Pies"(Lies) which circulates into intellectual propaganda and then people quote it as their gospel truths.

Throughout time, many people who behave without universal intelligence have contributed to evolving devastation and mayhem. The majority, personally do not destroy others, but they allow ignorance of the truth to fester as they buy into their artificial lifestyle. In time, a dictator or religious doctrine comes along to take advantage of a powerless, gullible society. It often takes a devastating war to get back and begin a new round of ignorance. In peace time, we just wreck our own immune systems with illusionary anxieties tied to our mistaken identities.

Mr. & Mrs. Humbug get sick quite often. They just dote on devouring large helpings of worry. The "lucky ones" who don't die of self-inflicted disease, are saved by medication and surgery, however their quality of life greatly diminishes.

When a mortal being acts only with ego's power, it forfeits the connection to their natural spiritual sense of living a fulfilling life. An empty life with no meaning, is a wasted existence, so why do folks insist on "Going it alone." Why endure hardship and suffering in a world that is constantly changing? Why live life in a stressful manner when every molecule and cell is constantly changing. The answer is simple but hard to find.

Mr. & Mrs. Humbug say life has treated them cruelly and cannot see the beauty that constantly encompasses them. They go into buildings to find God and pray for help. When they leave the building, they leave God behind. Being the good caretaker he is, God keeps the building in good shape. Mr. & Mrs. humbug do not recognize their bodies as Gods temple, so they can go into dis-repair. They can donate money for a building but cannot find the time to donate genuine in-sights to their true-selves.

Folks who cannot change the stale, worn out thoughts live in the clutches of ego's prison. If everything is constantly changing, why stick with the same thought pattern? What is so wonderful about worry and anxiety that we have to love and nurture it? Could it be our negativity has become our desired "normal" habits. More to the point, what is so wonderful about our notability, which was never of our choosing in the first place, that is worth keeping? If we possessed stockings that were full of holes, would we keep on wearing them?

Mr. and Mrs. Humbug are always poor of spirit, no matter how much money they accumulate. They have lost the desire to live natural as nature intended; consequently they exist within catastrophic normality.

We have become so attached to an identity that is masterly destructive, that we do not know how to let go of it. We are held captive by a master of havoc, who has hypnotized us into accepting self made lies. Yes indeed, ego = Ease God Out, is a BIG falsifier. It tells us all kinds of illusionary tales and we accept them as our truths. What's more, most of the folks we know also be-lie-ve the falsehoods. They are also hoodwinked by their master of havoc. The academy of egotism only turns out grade A students, brainwashed to obey a singular perception of life.

Mr. & Mrs. Humbug are dedicated followers of false images and tailor misconstrued thoughts. The latest media hype gets them all flustered leading to sleepless nights, bad digestion, encouraging the seeds of disease.

We have allowed a false identity to become our reference point to all the temporal things that surround us. We had no choice in accepting this identity, for it was transmitted to us by other folks, who were also living a false existence. Society has shaped itself on ideas that have no place in nature, except in ego's alien normality nature. It is very far removed from human nature, yet we call an alien human nature, human nature. We say it is only human nature to worry. It is only human nature to feel jealous and hate. No, No that is ego's nature, not human nature and it is a false devil and master. A baby must first 'grow up' before it can be taught how to hate.

Mr. & Mrs. Humbug Pray to the Holy Cow, The Stock Market, for deliverance to secure an advantageous lifestyle. If they succeed, they can then torment themselves in luxury rather than be tormented in poverty.

The alien ego-being, masquerading as a human being, be-lie-ves a real supernatural devil exists and does not understand that the ego itself is it's own devil. Some ego-devils are more openly destructive than others but all egos can contain illusionary devils, as long as the ego masters the mind. Human beings convictions are as real as the ego- beings devil control of the mind & body. In reality neither exists nor have any true, lasting power. The most an egos power can assemble is one lifetime of conflict in a human mind. A lifetime of hallucinations, living in ignorant grandeur. A primeval dynasty of primitive engagements, wrestling with themselves in a ring of thorns.

Mr. & Mrs. Humbug love to gossip, favor criticizing others and accommodate pet hates. Tittle-tattle may seem like a fun sport, however the ramifications to health and happiness suffer the consequences. The golden rule they forgot is; to do onto other as we would have done to us.

An ego _ being has no foundation or structure. It lives within the realms of a mirage and when trouble strikes the mirage is shattered. This leaves a broken hearted human forsaken, in a maze of confused thoughts...A nervous wreck on the brink of an early demise. Cancer and heart failure are just a couple of the many contributions from a stressful life, dwelling in worry and woes, will bring. Do we really want our ego to retain it's mastery over our minds?

Mr. & Mrs. Humbug endure an empty existence and leave without ever knowing the meaning of Joy. Sadly, on their death bed, they realize they cheated themselves of a life filled with love & joy, Alas, too late becomes the cry.

As long as ego/intellect holds court, all the slaves will obey. The period of ego's trademark of slavery is drawing to an end. The academy of egotism is about to go belly up. Bankrupted by its own greed for power. It may take a decade or two before freedom within clarity of thought and creativity commences. However, the time is fast approaching when the illusions of our societies will begin to disappear, either by a nuclear holocaust or more hopefully, an awakening connection to the divine fountain of truth.

We are about to harvest a change of thought patterns and an understanding of a higher reality. A change in our perception of life...A cleansing of old useless attachments, to be replaced with the surrender to the eyewitness within.

Mr. & Mrs. Humbug's eyewitness within has yet to be called to testify on the violations of universal laws. We will grasp our true psychology of life and start to gain wisdom in our schools and universities.

- We will procure and nurture wisdom with love and Joy, seeing it as a benchmark of real meaning.
- We will walk in harmony with all life forms and protect our mother earth.
- We will begin to give back to earth all we have taken.
- We will return to the divine world of serenity and tranquility.
- The new Academy of Wisdom is about to open its doors to all.
- The next generation of wise mortals are about to take center stage and show all the infinite possibilities the universe can teach. A crop of goodness awaits all who start to sow their seeds of wisdom.

Mr. & Mrs. Humbug only grow weeds in their psychological garden of self-delusions. The realizations of spirits truth will become paramount so that the weeds can mystically seed glorious blooms of de-light.

- Human beings are seeded from natures core values, allowing growth by natural intrinsic, intuitive intent.
- When we remain connected to natural nature, then our seeds will flourish and bloom.
- Earth is part of the universal flow and we are the children of the creator/evolver of earth.
- The Universal Spirit is asking us to tune in.
- The orchestrations have been composed.
- The music is playing delightful melodies.
- Now is the time to dance in step with nature.

Mr. & Mrs. Humbug are out of step with creation, they believe divine order is a slice of Pizza followed by ice cream.

- Only Spirit holds true joy and meaning, everything else are self-deceptions played on Mr. & Mrs. Humbug.
- When wisdom is fused with intellect, mankind progresses in a credible direction.

- All the greatest sages of the past have echoed the silent voice of their inner spirit.
- Our hearts desires are guided by the soul's intuitive power, embracing true Joy.
- We walk on a sacred, divinely guided thoroughfare.

When all is said and done, we are just passing through. Why not make every day and night, a joyful occasion, for celebrating the gift of life.

Everybody enters this world in innocence; however, most leave it in ignorance.

SLICE FIVE
Be-lie-ve Unsound Perceptions?

Many moons ago, human beings developed 'something' that allowed them to use their brain in a more sophisticated manner than all the other primates. We have past records of a time when humans were cave dwellers who learnt how to shape tools to create all types of useful utensils. Early hi-tech wonders were the making of fire and then the invention of the wheel.

Do you know the name of the man or woman who invented the wheel? If s/he had patented it, how much would that be worth in to-days world... Quite a bit more that the value of Microsoft I should imagine.

Well, there was no money in those days and people did things to help their community just for the good of each other. They were simple beings who enjoyed each sunrise, sunset and natures resplendent bounty with any distortion or distraction of an 'educated' intellectual mind. They required no reasons to enjoy life, for they were just glad to be alive.

Many great inventions took place when we were a primitive race of be-ings... Sharp stones on sticks (spears) to hunt game, cooking pots to cook the catch of the day and many other things that made life easier than previous generations. One thing led to another and another and another. Then wheel gave birth to faster land transport and boats meant man could venture forth throughout the world to plunder and pillage less sophisticated tribes.

The more intellectually sharp-witted a tribe became, the more power they learnt to consume, the more atrocious became their actions. Therefore, very early in human development, man learnt they could procure other peo-ples wealth by fighting wars. Indeed, it did not take long for people to learn not only could they steal and rape from other tribes, they could use various methods both violent and cunningly non-violent in extracting ill gotten gains from their own clan.

Laws are made-up and clever people learnt to bend the laws. Many times, it was the lawmakers themselves, who bend their own laws, for the leaders in power. The more the intellectual mind developed, the more demanding became its obsession with so-called power and wealth. More and more diabolical acts followed. The information that is recorded in history books is probably only the tip of the iceberg, in all the injustices done to different populations throughout the ages.

Why? … Was the question asked, by many of the six million Jews, who walked into the gas chambers?

Why? … Was the question asked by native Americas when mans greed annihilate whole families whist they seized their land?

Why? … Was the question asked by Mayan civilizations that were butchered by the Spanish conquistadors in the name of religion and conquest?

Why? … Was the question asked when thirty million people were killed in the First World War?

Why? … Was the question asked, in 2001 when the twin towers and four airplanes filled with passengers were destroyed by Muslim fundamentalists?

Why? …Why? …Why? … and a zillion more whys, in every human life, since man became a sophisticated thinker.

Maybe the answer lies in our own tribes, in our own societies, in our own countries.

So the question now becomes.

Why do clever people be-lie-ve in so many unsound perceptions of what life is all about? Ralph Waldo Emerson said; *"It is hard to be simple enough to be good."* and so it is. If humanity were not so clever, they would not be able to invent so many tools of destruction and decimation. In addition, the "Haves" would not be able to manufacture so many luxury items to tempt the 'Have-nots' or the "Want-mores" from stealing them. But, what causes the crimes and wars?

Is it the materialism itself that cause people to commit crimes, or is it in-built jealousy, greed, avarice, hatred and a whole host of clever erroneous evil thought?

Yep! Humanity certainly has to be clever intellectually to be able to project its ignorance to the masses, or how else will they be able to hate so many people. That kind of inaccurate intellectual thinking must lack a magnitude of intelligence, because intelligent people, with wisdom, seldom get disconnected from their source of creation/evolving... Thus have no need to commit crimes of greed and hate.

You certainly have to teach students how to read and write, but without the true reasons why they are learning intellectual skills, they can perfect ways to become swindlers and cheats. Golden rule... You can cheat and swindle innocent people, but you must not get found out and if you do get found out... Mums the word...The old school tie, don't you know old chap...Lets all stick together.

"What does education often do? It makes a straight-cut ditch of a free, meandering brook."
_Henry David Thoreau

Bending laws is so much fun for the twisted educated swindlers in all of society's establishments. It becomes a game of who can out-think the other rivals, who are also in positions of power... Trying to find additional, better methods of cheating innocent folks...Bankers, brokers, corporations executives, religious leaders, politicians, etc, etc, etc. All of bent and twisted unsound thinkers need one thing in common, to succeed in deceiving innocent people... What was it they all required, to be so cunningly clever?

They All needed a good unsound education, filled with unsound perceptions of life!

All taught by unsound education systems that lacked true purpose, objectivity and balance.

"Education is an admirable thing, but it is well to remember from time to time that nothing worth knowing can be taught." _Oscar Wilde

Many academic degrees were award to many students. But no degrees-of-wisdom were handed out...How could there be? Who is there teaching in the universities that understands the true meaning of life and how to combine it in all subjects? Educating students should not be solely a scholastic application. Whilst it is true there are many advancements in many fields such as medicine and science, humanity in terms of genuine happiness and serenity, is worse off today then it was thousands of years ago. Advancement in knowledge should not mean a slide in joy, so why is it we have such a web of ignorance in academia?

"There is nothing so stupid as the educated man if you get him off the thing he was educated in." _Will Rogers

Natural intelligence is the mastery primitive man used to feed their intellects in order to prosper...In today's world, the intellect replaces natural universal intelligence by virtue of an inflated ego. It then tries to invent new intelligent systems, modes, mental conditioning, that seem clever, chic and sensible, but is no more that a bunch of erroneous, synthetic, pointless theories.

How many teachers and professors are centered and balanced, do not have any partisan one-sided political associations and not an ounce of hatred or jealously in them?

How many teachers and professors do not try to protect their turf and their academic understanding of the word... truthfulness?

How many headmasters, deans and professors in academia are open, to at least listen, to the simple, authentic meaning of life, which did not stem from the proud words contained in the textbooks of academia?

How many universities do not have a political leaning to the left or the right?

If all the teaching in university textbooks is sound, why are the headlines of the newspapers packed, with scandalous goings-on and heinous actions, in every area of human society?

"We are students of words: we are shut up in schools, and colleges, and recitation-rooms, for ten or fifteen years, and come out at last with a bag of wind, a memory of words, and do not know a thing." _Ralph Waldo Emerson

Do you really want to know why clever people be-lie-ve in so many unsound thoughts. Ask a analytical academic person if they know when universal intelligence comes from. If they don't know the sources of wisdom, all we will get is clever people with many unsound ideas. In addition, a society that continues to live in ignorance of the true facts of life... Maybe it's time for humanity to understand the birds and the bees a little better. How a caterpillars metamorphic transformation into butterfly is done with no academic skills. No intellectual reasoning can better that type of real live alchemy.

On both sides of the debate between religion v science there are many bigoted and dogmatic people who be-lie-ve they have the power to control others. Absolute truth evades the intellectual mind and at best most people live with Perceptions, Ideas, Thoughts, Suggestions... And there my friend is the reason humanity is in the PITS.

SLICE SIX
The Masterly Art of Stupidity

We live in a stupid world filled with oceans of stupidity in every area of human existence... For example; the world financial markets have been taken close to a meltdown by clever experts who devised leveraged financial instruments that very few people understood and yet they bought them for a higher yield. Everyone involved had one thing in common, what was it I can hear you ask... they all had a good education. Even now, if you ask them, none will admit they are stupid. They will paper over the cracks and admit to making some mistakes and will make amends in the future.

Until a person can call themselves stupid (without blaming themselves for their stupidity) an authentic life will elude them. This statement may horrify those folks who are intellectually fed and lead, however, if their intellect is not controlled by their innocent intelligence (and very few are) they will continue to live out ignorant stupidness, without ever recognizing it for what it is.

To become a success, we really need to learn how to become a master in the art of stupidity in an intelligent manner. Understand, there are two forms of being stupid. One which I do not recommend is filled with ignorance of the fact that stupidity is part of the daily make-up and this type of person only lives by intellectual thoughts that have been handed down over thousands of years of collective rules and regulations. Their stubborn egotistical nature leads them into all types of pitfalls.

The other type of stupidity which I do subscribe to is... not buying into ones own smartness and questioning all A-ctions, T-houghts, C-leverness, before they ACT.

Because I have been called stupid all my life, by people who deemed themselves to be clever, I guess I can award myself the highest degree of stupidity in every aspect of living.

If we cannot recognize our own stupidity then we will rely on our intellectual cleverness to work things out for us and the results will rarely produce a successful life on earth, even though society may view it as successful.

Remember, stupidity has two sides to it. One side is self evident by humanities erroneous actions and events since the beginning of cleverness without a true guiding light. This form of stupidly be-lie-ves it has mastered stupidity, yet all the results say otherwise. Therefore they have become a slave to their own stupidity and disguise it with flawed systems and policies that herd mentalities accept as normal ways to live.

The other side to stupidity is the simple mindedness that identifies itself and thus can overrule its cleverness, so that it can make better choices. This type of stupidity has been embraced by every sage and person of wisdom since the beginning of time. In their day they were mostly executed or tortured for their so called stupidity and yet it has stood the test of time.

Most people live in an intellectual zoo locked into a cage of their own self-cleverness. Some try to attract other to join their be-lie-fs by writing a book or giving a lecture. Some may be reward for their antics with tasty morsels like awards or accolades. I suppose not too many people would be happy living in a zoo and yet so many do live locked in a mind-set of imprisonment, caught in a cage of perceptions, ideas, thoughts and suggestions (PITS). A be-lie-f system that completely overwhelms the conscious brain very rarely changes its outlook on life.

The awareness of my own stupidity allows me to live in comfortable contentment.

SLICE SEVEN
The Ten Advantages of
Intelligent Stupidity

1/ We allow ourselves time for closer inspection of important decision making and restrict our ego/intellect from taking hold of the conscious mind.

2/ We do not allow our own cleverness to take us on a wild ride that may seem fruitful, yet on closer inspection we realize, the consequences of our actions may not be the outcome we desire.

3/ When other people say we are stupid we can agree with them and then they have nothing left to attack us with.

4/ Once we can acknowledge our own stupidly other peoples absurdities becomes obvious. Wise folks learn from other peoples mistakes.

5/ Forewarned is forearmed... By living in the center of our stupidly we can see the dangers that lurk before we act out our roles and thus guide ourselves on a more simple route through life's mazes...Which in turn guides to live an amazing life.

6/ Expert advice is examined far more closely and nothing is taken for granted.

7/ By understanding our stupidity, our awareness of dangers takes on greater might and alerts us to risks more clearly.

8/ It is not only wars and conflicts that are foolhardy, it is also unnecessary risks taken in peace time such as climbing a mountain in a blizzard that bring about an early demise. Stupid people will not attempt to take on nature as they do not possess the ego that makes them think they are mightier than God.

9/ Stupid people understand all negative emotions are illusions and thus not real. Therefore their immune system is not open to stress. However, all the clever learned people, who teach us how to mange stress, are open to the negative emotions they are trying to control.

10/ By living out our daily stupidity in a joy filled mind, we find more success in better health, greater wealth, and abundant happiness. Also, we do not overestimate our power to change anyone.

What works will prove itself and what doesn't work will testify to the clever, stupid ignorance of a misguided society.

Certainty and uncertainty wear the same persona under differing guises and you can be certain of the uncertainty.

SLICE EIGHT
Flying Posthaste Into Human Destruction.

The more we study nature and all the magnificent variety of creatures it assembles, the more we can understand and appreciate how our minds and bodies function. The more we comprehend the character our world has been molded by human ignorance, the more we can observe where we are heading as a species. It appears as though humanity is flying posthaste into a force field of self destruction.

One of the most fascinating creatures that exist on earth are a group of birds that have similarities to the actions of humans in a most definite way. The species are called "Bower birds"

The male Bower bird is a skilled artist and creator of elaborate designs. Scientists have been studying these birds for a long time with great interest. They were featured on a nature program on PBS that caught my attention and fascinated my curiosity. It was narrated by David Attenborough who is a genius in the study of nature. The whole point of the Bower bird's exotic behavior is to attract a female for mating.

Unlike peacocks and many other birds that show off their plumage, this bird needs to construct a Bower of intricate design on the floor of the forest from leaves, moss and twigs. It then bedecks the bower with showy trinkets such as stones, beetle shells, feathers, berries, flowers and all fashions of decorative "ornaments." Many times it will also construct a canopy for the female bird to walk through which resembles a canopy that can be found at a Jewish wedding. It is decorated with all kinds of objects the bird can pick up from its surroundings. It also steals objects from neighboring male Bower birds and will furthermore attempt to destroy the other bird's bower. This has two purposes. It lessens the other bird's chances to attract a mate and it enhances its own Bower. (Does this sound familiar to human behavior?)

Eventually a female will show up to check out the quality of the bower. It is then the male goes into a ritual of struts and song. The plainer the bird, the more elaborate the Bower, but the more colorful the birds plumage, the less creative are their Bowers. The whole object of the male Bowers life is to woe a mate by creative construction that can only come from an intelligence source far greater than the little pea brain the little bird possess. Despite being surrounded by the beauty of nature that most other birds enjoy, The Bower bird's sole interest is his small area of self made creation. (Does this sound familiar to the close mindedness of most partitions and divisions in society?)

The similarities to human behavior cannot be denied. Most intellectual people seem to believe human beings are somehow or other a special one off breed, which is aloof from other species and nothing, could be further from the truth. The cost of this ignorance is confirmed in all areas of human existence.

Every living "thing" accesses intelligence from a universal energy field. This is known as a unified energy source. However, each life force possesses a unique identity formed and evolved by their own surroundings and needs for survival. Many species evolved in a manner that seemed quite normal for them, but it was not as nature intended, it was not natural and their normal behavior designated them to extinction well before the natural life plan was enacted.

In the development of all specie there are two paths to follow. One path is enhanced by an awareness of universal laws that continues to blossom and savors the delightful treasures of existence. The other is a narrow-minded avenue of survival that does not always follow universal laws and tries to reformulate the master blueprints of nature. They do appear get away with it for quite a while, but eventually they go so far removed from the grand architects plans that their foundations crumble. The results are after many generations of mayhem the species becomes extinct too soon.

The Bower bird's attachment to objects could become so acute that the female may evolve to the state of mind that no Bower is good enough for her. Therefore she will cease to mate with the male and the species will become extinct.(Not tonight dear, I have a headache) This may also happen if the males become too aggressive in building their Bowers and start to not only steal from other males, but attack and kill them (Does this sound familiar?)

Humans have evolved into a sophisticated species that contain both positive and negative intellectual thoughts, but it is the negative aspects of life that holds court with in the psyche. It seems the modern day mortal is dying far too soon because of stress related dis-ease. Cancer, heart disease, diabetes and a host of other ailments all come from attachments to an inauthentic actuality. The medical profession is trying to patch up our frail systems with medications and surgery. The medical patchwork quilt treats the effects of our addictions, but can do nothing to stop our relentless evolving into a self destructive mode of living.

The Bible is a good place to find the cause of our self destructive path. It all started when Adam took a bite out of the apple from the Tree of Knowledge. This is symbolic because the human intellect established identification with the "things" it could create, instead of remaining connected with the genuine source of creation. Humanity was in big trouble and the reference point of thought became the artificial world of attachment to materialism.

Humans beings began to evolve in a normal man made manner that the intellect approved, but ceased to exist in a natural manner that the creator approved.

The continuation of egotistical thinking over a 30,000 year period has given humans a DNA and genes that are programmed in a way that will lead to mortal destruction. Unless we can change the pattern of misguided thinking by reconstructing our thought process and patterns, we are condemned into the self disintegration of humanity. The hi-tech revolution with all its weaponry, along with the sham world of egoistical thinking, will become moralities demise. We are children playing with mis-matches of beliefs that will explode the hell fires of annihilation.

We are akin to the bower birds, but alas we have "progressed" down a slippier slope of the human intellect and the grip is far too tight to be release. It is a bull dog grip that is locked into a mode of living that cannot contain its power for greed and its entrapment in fear. Humans have built a bower that is sinking into the bowels of the earth... In other worlds...Humanity is being flushed down the Toilet by mis-conditioned thinking!!

There is only one true high-way out of the dark shadows of the egotism. But there are many paths to sink humanity further into the mire.

Unfortunately there are only but a handful of humans who know the way towards the light, bright, Joy filled life, but they are ridiculed by society in general. They are also ignored by science and religion, for each sector believes it must maintain its own power base, or it will disappear. Most organizations are being paid large amounts of money from divided segments of the community who live in ignorance of authentic meaning. The chances of them accepting a higher reality of living is not an option they will readily consider. Dogmas and doctrines still hold the power to suppress authentic meaning.

We are all living in the Garden of Eden right now. We live in utopia, paradise, heaven on earth. People who cannot see that only add to the self destruction of Humanity. Will the Bower bird survive its attachment to ornaments and trimmings rather than nature? Will humans survive their attachments to the catastrophic forces of negative emotion?

At this moment in time it looks unlikely humanity can stop itself from a major calamity within a very short time span. Unless the few humans that live an authentic natural lifestyle are acknowledged and their philosophy respected, "normality" will sentence the lambs to the slaughter.

Ask yourself...Is it time to start to live a life of J-O-Y every second the clock ticks...Just - Obey - Yourself...Your true self...Not the intellectual that holds the matches to light the fires of devastation.

The Ego that holds the chain of command will be the power that flushes humanity back into the Bowels of the earth.

Well, let's at least look at the good side of human extinction... It will allow the Bower birds to pick up all the ornamental human remains and make a beautiful, exquisite Bower.

The true beholder exists in the eye of beauty.

SLICE NINE
A Birds Eye View of Life

There is an old saying, which goes *"we should live life as free as a bird"* but do all birds live a free life? Another question we may ask is "do birds possess some form of ego?" If so, then perhaps their life is not as free as it seems.

A few years ago, I was watching an enthralling display by birds of prey in the glorious South of England. It was fascinating to see how owls and falcons are trained to fly around an open field, and then land on different stations and posts when called. How magnificent they are when they swoop in to seize food from a swinging rope. All was going well until they brought out the star of the show. This was a falcon with its own strong mind and would do things in its own time.

The falcon came out and flew way up high in the sky. It circled our area for a few minutes and just when it seemed to be sweeping down to take its prey swinging on the end of a rope, it decided it was enjoying its freedom and headed up even higher and more distant. The trainer told us the falcon was entering in a space that is protected by two Peregrine falcons. She stated that their falcon would be attacked and chased off for flying in the Peregrines space. The Peregrines had no young in their nest; hence they were protecting what they believed is "their hunting ground"

Well, I began to think, if a bird protects its air space then they must have an idea of their identity. If they have an identity, then maybe they possess some type of an ego, for only an ego thinks it holds possessions. The two Peregrines believe they own their patch of sky, therefore other birds were not free to fly in their territory. I do not know how many type of birds protect their patch of sky, but all birds protect their nest and that seems to be a rational instinct to protect life and not egotistical.

Protecting a nest is a natural action to preserve life, but to extend that instinct to protect the sky seems to be one of selfishness. The question is, have some birds of prey evolved to act in an aggressive manner, so that they can possess their air space? Are they mistakenly thinking they need to protect their space in order to survive? Even though there was open countryside all around, filled will all types of small tasty creatures they eat, this small patch of sky was theirs! It seems as if it had become "normal" for these birds to act aggressively to protect their patch of sky.

The trainer's falcon did not stay in the Peregrines space for too long, as it must have a good memory of past attacks it had encountered. Within a few seconds, it flew away, far beyond our view and was out of sight for half an hour or more. This falcon was truly as free as a bird now and the whole of the surrounding countryside was his domain.

Quite suddenly it came back into our sight and within a few minutes came whizzing over our heads (within a few inches) and swooped on its pray which was a dead mouse on the end of the twirling rope. What a fascinating display, via a bird's eye view of life, we observed that day.

How many of us live as an egotistical birdbrain? To put it another way, how many people protect the space between their ears that stores a man made belief system? We all grow up to accept a belief system or political viewpoint. Now what happens when some newcomer comes into our life and invades our space of thought with a differing viewpoint? Many dogmatic, egotistical people will not tolerate anyone else's point of view from entering their thoughts, so they immediately attack. They find many ways of aggressively fending off any opinion that could threaten their own territory. On a more obstreperous scale, a war of words turns into a military war of destruction and mayhem. Are we no better than a bird, with a brain the size of a pea?

Do we really need to go through life with a limited view of our beliefs, or should we open up our skies (minds) and fly all around the universe to acquire new and exciting original thoughts? The trainers falcon was free to fly where he wished once let off the lead. He flew high and wide and enjoyed his freedom. But he came home to a loving master after his free flight.

Fifty-thousand years ago, humans began to transform from natural beings and evolved into sophisticated, complex, tangled beings. Humans evolved intellectually whist at the same time forfeiting much of their natural biological identity. Today our normality is creating havoc and mayhem all around the world, in our everyday lives. Can we return to a more natural life and still enjoy all the modern day trappings?

We live but a brief life on earth, whereby we have been let out to roam free and think at will. We only have a short period to fly freely because we are just passing though on our eternal journey. Let's not restrict our space to think. It has become "normal" for the ego to protect its viewpoints. The spirit will fly freely... Naturally, (natures rally) with an open mind. Whom do you want to fly with today?

There are so many new creative ideas we can swoop on, to help society free itself from captivity of egotistical thoughts. We may not possess a bird's eyesight or hearing abilities, but surely we can think a little clearer than a contentious, out of tune birdbrain... or can we? The intellect is not the source. Tradition is not the source. However, the source can become the intellects tradition.

Slow down enough to build a canopy of joy over the time you inhabit.

SLICE TEN
A Kaleidoscope of Energy

All animals function by various aspects of energies that embody intelligence. Every species on earth possess their own natural, special instincts and intuitions that keep them clear of danger. It also helps them to find the food and water they need to survive on a sometimes-hostile planet.

The human animal is a kaleidoscope of energy infused with the intelligence of the universe, which can reason its own existence. It can distinguish decent, respectable behavior from offense, outrageous conduct and by implementing sensible laws of the land that keep their society in a principled state of vitality. This should make humanity more caring and civilized then all the other animals, but as everyone knows, that is not always the case... So what is it that make a human being tick?

In every human body and mind, billions of particles are constantly forming and reforming. They are held in a time & space mode, for approximately three hundred earth seasons... The time span on average in today's world is around seventy-five years. Only one and three quarter percent live past eighty-five. The intelligence emanating from the minds of modern medical scientists is extending the human life-span, but are they enriching them?

The human being is evolving and creating new ideas in an ever-changing landscape of unity and confusion. With the free will to act in a random manner, as a self serving individual, intent on avariciously grabbing a bigger share of earths abundant pie than needed.

Or, to behave in a unified manner, sharing their natural, loving gifts of nature with all their community. Both the unified and the random acts encompass intelligence and will lead to an ultimate destination of what dualistic observes class as good and bad.

When separate indoctrinations and dogmas are the guidelines in a community, it usually induces suffering and sorrow on everyone in that country and can affect world peace.

On the other side of the see-saw, when everyone is united with the same universal truths that do not contain any divisions... Where everyone can agree on a connected, progressive agenda, the result is a joyful harmonious community, living a fulfilling and meaningful life.

"Just as a stream flows smoothly on as long as it encounters no obstruction, so the nature of man and animal is such that we never really notice or become conscious of what is agreeable to our will; if we are to notice something, our will has to have been thwarted, has to have experienced a shock of some kind." _Arthur Schopenhauer

Our Mind & Body is a replica of the universe and once we study ourselves beyond human selfish, egotistical thinking, we find answers to everything we need, to live unified, as nature deems possible...We enter a field of pure potential, where feelings and sensations expand in an infinite sphere beyond mere words and actions. When we magnify the human potential by the infinite possibilities nature allocates, the resulting outcome becomes clear for all to see. Great works of art, music, writing, architecture, scientific discovers, business, etc., blossom and bloom as radiant exquisite monuments to human creativity.

Therefore, when we live as a unified force in a structured society, there is no conflict or confusion. Alternatively, when we act solely in an egotistical manner, our power base explodes into haphazard actions and destroys. So there is uncertainty on one hand and unification on the other.

Humanity is shaped by a universal intelligence that is a mirror image of the whole of the universe. Einstein said; space & time creates the universe in which stars have planets, which circle them in predictable ways.... "A Unified Theory." Our mind and body is in constant movement as the life blood flows through each vein and artery ... we call that ... circulation. All parts of the mind/body need to be in unified circulation to function properly.

When there is disharmony, parts of the mind and body cease to function in an orderly manner and disease, followed by an early death, is the result ... This becomes.... "The Uncertainty Theory," which is also scientifically explained by the random actions of various particles out in space. Both theories are scientific, both theories contradicting each other and yet both are correct.

The mind of the universe can act in a random unpredictable manner when it ignores its own intelligence. The intelligence is always there, it just isn't always followed, for like humans, it to has its own free will to act randomly, absent of its own intelligence.

Turmoil and disarray explode in seemingly unpredictable actions.

When the random energy expires and the chaotic acts cease, new matter forms emerge from intelligence, that were not planed in the original unity blueprints.

Random and Unified will always exist side by side. Evolving and creating new forms of matter. When random acts destroy newly formed matter, it will be replaced by new formations and then existing in a time span that will "age"... Destruction and decimation is always followed by construction and clarification. Everything follows a natural flowing process.

Nothing in a particle form lasts... All stars eventually burn out and explode taking planets and all matter with them. Then they transform into the gasses from which they were created. They are then sucked into a dimension called a "Golden Hole" of extreme light, covered by darkness science refers to as a black hole When large amounts of gases are compressed into the light spectrum, their darkness begins to conflict with the intense light, a large spark, which we call a big bang, pushes the gasses out of the blackness so that they form a fresh, original universe, that establishes new matter particles...

The universe is in darkness, however the gasses and particles have been infused with light from the "Golden Hole," and will eventually form larger particles of matter... The particles will swirl in clusters and adhere to each other, then ignite as stars, which in turn will form planets....

Time has no meaning until living intelligent forms of matter takes on a human shape. After billions of years our earth was formed and four billion years later the first humans walked on earth and time began. Before that, as far as humans understand, no other life forms recognized time as a reality...

"Animals have these advantages over man: they never hear the clock strike, they die without any idea of death, they have no theologians to instruct them, their last moments are not disturbed by unwelcome and unpleasant ceremonies, their funerals cost them nothing, and no one starts lawsuits over their wills." _Voltaire.

Today, humans should follow the natural flow of nature and be aware of the dangers and pitfalls a hostile planet can produce... Such as tsunamis or earthquakes. Other animals are intrinsically aware of natures devastation's and can escape the dangers unharmed. It seems humans have lost that inherent power. Humanity has filled its mind in sophisticated thinking that has altered its orderly circulation and thus limited its awareness of natural devastation signals.

When humans ignore danger signals that could produce random destruction, many lives are lost. Humanities intelligent energy does not operate as originally planned. Their intellect/ego has become the victims of random energy. Unbalanced humans, devoid of intrinsic essentials are destroyed by the performance of unbalances acts of nature......It really is quite simple. Because we put a value on life, we see things that destroy as a disaster and yet this is the way our universe functions. If human intelligence has been numbed by sophisticated living, then the consequences will be dire.

Humanity has to face a sporadic hostile environment and at the same time has to cope with its own sporadic wars and conflicts... Oh! what an intricate web of perils humanity weaves... Once it learns to re-think and deceive.

"I have been studying the traits and dispositions of the "lower animals" (so called) and contrasting them with the traits and dispositions of man. I find the result humiliating to me."
_Mark Twain

If we eat the wrong foods and stress our bodies with the wrong thoughts, our bodies will adapt to a free radical approach; the free radicals destroy our bodies. When our minds focus on a free radical approach to life, many conflicts and wars pursue. If we use intelligence and wisdom in our daily lives, along with Intellect and Ego, we find a blissful contentment. We are guided to eat the correct foods, exercise and think happy thoughts; we unify with the Universe and live in peace and harmony.

We can enhance Earth and progress to make the whole of the Universe a place where physical life can exist in a joy filled state of well being. We all have our part to play, for we are all part of the Big Picture. Take a look in the mirror and Smile. We are a reflection of the Universe. Spirit gave us the Joy of life, Let's not waste it. A Smile travels an Infinite distance, to be greeted by Love and beauty.

Conclusion.

If we live a life of anguish filled with worry and fear; If we hold jealousy and hatreds and are quick to anger; Then we live as a random particle of energy, detached from the whole unified field of energy. A single unit of energy, born to endure hardship, which will cause sadness and effect all the folks we meet. Our lives will be spent in regret, guilt and remorse and death will be our final release. We will then become united once again but we would have wasted our lives.

If we live within a united force field and allow the intelligence of Spirit to guide our daily events in a calm peaceful manner; To love and find beauty in all we see; To enjoy every second on earth; We will cause health, wealth and happiness to abound in glorious profusion, which will effect a feeling of well being to all we meet and greet. We will never feel alone and in silence we will become one with the whole of the Universe. Charging our energy with Spirits Power. We will live as God intended. In a Majestic Grace of Love and Joy.

Diamond white Joy, Crystal light Love ... Illuminations projecting true success

SLICE ELEVEN
A Jolly Green God

Many conservative Evangelical Christians are going green ... Not with jealousy but with environment issues such as global warming and pollution. They believe Gods word in the bible that states human beings are the guardians of his all his creations on earth, and that includes mother earth. They are taking up the good fight to protect the planet and prolong the human lifespan in a healthy state of being

What are the issue humanity faces that do not allow most human beings the chance to blow out the candles on their hundredth birthday cake? Statistics state not too many people live past the age of eighty. Many trees and plants have a far more prolonged life than human beings ... Indeed; there are a multitude of animals, fish and birds that have a longer life span.

- Animals, birds and fish can live without getting sick and going to a doctor for pills.
- Could it be our intelligence mixed up in a conceited maze of ignorance?
- Could it be we really do not need to die a premature death from disease?
- Do we have no option other than to declare, there is no other choice than intermittent illness throughout our lifetime, leading to an early grave?

A few people do live to a ripe old age because they inherited strong genes and DNA. However, leaving that aside, how does the average person live in good health, to a fully developed old age, as nature intended?

I guess most folks believe that our 'advancements' in the world of science and medicine have increased our life expectancy. This is true to some extent, but it is only true in the context of keeping us alive in ill health, despite our continuous bad habits and erroneous lifestyles. We can alleviate the effects of an illness, but the cause lingers on, bringing with it an uncomfortable life that eventually leads to a premature, uncomfortable passing. So what can be done to remedy the situation of being a pawn in a commercial chess game of beggar thy neighbor, performed in a worldwide playhouse?

Firstly, if we stop polluting the earth with poisonous gasses, pesticides and a multitude of other pollutants we would need fewer drugs to sustain our lives. Therefore, it seems sensible to stop corporations from manufacturing pollutants because of their need to feed the greed of a few humans, who hold stocks in their companies.

In addition, self-pollution is an outstanding problem and banning poisonous smoking in all public places, inside and outdoors, is a must-do and long overdue action that is beginning to sprout wings in many Western counties.

The next move in the appropriate direction to a longer healthier life would be to educate folks on the correct foods to eat and liquids to drink. Pure water should be the principal drink and alcohol consumption should be restricted to three glasses of wine a week at the most.

Simple yet delicious whole foods, herbs and spices that are heart healthily and loved by every cell in our bodies can supply all our dietary needs.

Our minds are constantly brainwashed by the advertising media educating our taste buds to enjoy refined foods contain high levels of sugar, salt, hydrogenated fats and other harmful "tasty stuff." These foods are usually all dressed up with colorants and artificial flavors. What a concoction of poison we have produced for ourselves. We pay good money to eat foods that bring about illness, which inconveniently installs us in a box six foot under the ground; before our shelf life was due to expire.

Simple regular exercise can be significant in helping to diminish the onset of many diseases. Walking and swimming are two of the easiest and most enjoyable forms of exercise available to most folks. A few weight-bearing exercises are also useful to keep muscle tone and bone strengthening.

However, the most important ingredient by far in living a long and healthy life is the way we think. What we need to ask ourselves is "Who is it that resides inside my head that makes all the decisions for me." If our minds have become too refined, just like the refined junk foods that we eat ... that has the wholesome goodness removed ... we could be left with junk-intellectual- thoughts ... Sophisticatedly refined, but good for nothing with real value ... A strong spiritual soul will never allow that to happen.

Once we start to recognize the true soulful genius that we authentically are ... that lives outside our ego's perceptions and opinions ... we will start to change our way of thinking and will live to the maximum of our allotted life-span. It could well be we live to 120 years of age in good health, if we do not allow negative, erroneous thoughts to upset the balance that nature has so magnificently provided for us all.

If we could only come to realize that we are a cog in the wheel of nature and if we desire that wheel to keep on turning effortlessly, we must become one with all that exists on earth.

The sands of time in humanities hourglass is quickly running out and unless we make the correct lifestyle changes, there will not be any life left here on earth for future generations to enjoy. So let human beings take a leaf out of the book of the Giant Tortoise and slow down the run-away greedy human brain. Let us all enjoy our lifetime swim in Gods delightful oceans of pure water, gardens of sweet fragrance flowers and beautiful green pastoral meadows.

First the word, then the deed, but what seeds, deceptive weeds?

SLICE TWELVE
Asleep in a bed of Fallacies

Has there ever been a time when humanity was united as one breed of nature, all assisting one another's progress, growth and prosperity? What is it that takes a new born baby on a journey of a lifetime into arguments, fights and wars? What breeds hatred and jealousy? What are the causes of fear and greed? Well, the answer simple put is, it is fallacies contained within the human brain....And, inside in the mortal brain dwells personal perceptions and assumptions of what life on earth is meant to be.Let's examine what a fallacy means, for it may shine some light on what we accept as our personal truths.

A fallacy is a fault in reason and logic of the intellectual mind. It is also a flaw in the human minds understanding and comprehension of realty, in the authentic sense of looking beyond a three dimensional world. Here are a few out of multitudinous fallacies that human's beings live with on a daily basis:

- Begging The Question;-going round in circles again and again and getting nowhere.
- Argumentum ad misericordiam; This is the Appeal to Pity, The fallacy is enacted when someone appeals to pity for the sake of getting a favorable decision accepted... He was mistreated and abused as a child so that's why he is a thief and a murderer.
- False Dilemma;- also known as the Black or White Fallacy...meaning there can only be two possibilities to the dispute.
- Post Hoc Fallacy;- communicating cause and effect must be an outcome of only two connections and no other outside event is involved. When one occurrence follows another, they may or may not be connected.
- Argumentum Ad Ignorantiam;-A statement that is regarded as truth merely because nobody can authenticate it beyond doubt...... Both

scientific and religious expressions, adopted by dogmatic minds, are very skilled at projecting this fallacy.

- Argumentum Ad Hominem;- vocally assaulting and insulting the person rather than the comments that you are attempting to cast doubt...Many times this verbal engagement can turn violent

- Reification;- This is when you assign life-like qualities to inanimate objects like stone or wood....However, rocks and trees all contain intelligence that the logical, egotistical mind cannot accept.

- Argumentum ad numerum;- A fallacy that exists in maintaining that the more people who support or believe a proposition, the more likely it is that proposition is correct...If everyone believes the world is flat, then it must be flat.

- Hypothesis Contrary To Fact;- using the imagination of events that may never have happened to prove the point.

- And in conclusion one of my own made up fallacies.......

- Post hicum-stickum ad intellecyuos ignoramousous fallacy;- This is when close-minded intellects try to ignore and reject the authentic soul, because they live only in a world governed by an out-of-tune mind fed by the ego!

And that my friends is how humankind removed themselves out of the Garden of Eden to live in a world that is ruled by the intellectual mind (the only place in the universe where evil exists)

And what evil we have in the world today. Children playing Suicide bomber games, only the TNT is real and they blow themselves up, along with innocent people.

- Terrorists that are intent on the destruction of all tribes who will not obey what they be-lie-ve to be their Gods directives.

- Corporations that steal billions of dollars from all their own people so that they can possess trophy homes, along with a false trophy life of luxuries.

- Government statistics that shade over precise fact and figures and lead people to believe things are better than they actually are.

- Advertising media that use fallacies to the extreme to benefit the chosen few with deep pockets who pay their wages of insincerity.
- Reality TV programs that accentuate the greed and fear fallacies. Movies that project horror, negative emotions and all things erroneous. Video games for children that emit terror, panic and alarm.... Dare I mention religion?

There has been, and still is, enough fallacies on earth, that if we strung them all out, they would reach beyond our solar system.

Now, there is just one question you need to ask yourself and nobody needs to hear your reply...How many fallacies do you hold in your mind and what are you going to do about them?

If you are looking for some guidelines that will provide you with a way of releasing unwanted conditioning of the mind, the solution is simple. Where can you find simple? ... Observe a new born baby. Or observe a flower.... Observe a rock....Observe anything that does not have the capacity to hold negative emotions....Just become aware of your own soul-source-of-energy.

Once you awaken from your living nightmares and get out of your bed of unfavorable fallacies, you will partake in many pleasant day time dreams... Well, most folks around you will think your dreaming, but in true essence, you are living in an authentic world, designed for you to inhabit, in a joy-filled mind...and what a great in-habit it truly is.

Remember...No matter how eloquently and articulately a dung heap is described; it will always be a dung heap.

SLICE THIRTEEN
Spiritual Franchisee.

Your reality is relative to the way your ego personality perceives life to be or not to be. The more you pay homage to your ego's singular view of life, the more likely it will be that you will live an unnatural life on earth. However, if you keep your ego's mind open and free, you will be able to distinguish falsehoods of meager intellectual facts from a truer reality that emanates from pulsating vibrations of intelligent, creative intelligence.

Experienced growers of fruit trees recognize the difference in the taste of fruit that is picked before it has matured and fruit that is perfectly ripe. They know not to pick the fruit from the tree until the fruit is ripe. If they wait until the wind blows the fruit from the tree and gather it right away, they would be eating the finest, most delicious, nutritious, sweetest fruit in all the land.

The question is; do you want to get your spiritual nourishment from second hand sources or do you want to get your spiritual communications right from the source.

You have the chance to enlist your mind into the service of your creator/ evolver every moment you are on earth. To establish the contact between you physical ego self and your origin of creation, you will need to spend a few minutes each morning and evening with a untroubled, quiet mind. The universal intelligence of a master-crafts-being will speak to you in a silent voice. It will transmit vibrational messages to your ego personality the opportunity to release its damaging hold on your body and mind so that it can love itself without conditioned restrictions. The silent voice of your trustworthy founder will instruct your intellect/ego to embrace the universal intelligence that connects love & joy into the human subconscious brain, thus communicating divine bliss into every cell of the human being.

Once you donate your valuable few minutes of time and become connected to your maker, you will feel the divine bliss of the tranquil communication.

You will then be given a choice that will allow you to tune into the high frequency channel of communication whenever your heart desires. By sharing your experience with everyone you meet and greet, your spiritual franchise will multiply in number and you will be serving your true purpose of good intent and peace on earth... Become a Free spiritual franchisee of your original architect's spirit. Once you make the correct connection you will start to build up you spiritual point. Your rewards will flow into your mind and the treasures of the universe will be yours to enjoy forever and a day!

If we only function as one droplet outside an ocean of thought, we will evaporate far too soon. It is far more preferable to free-style in the swim of the universe.

Even on the dullest days, simple souls, bask in rays of glory.

SLICE FOURTEEN
Cruise For Fun. Time-Out for a light humorous interlude.

I have often found that the funniest experiences in life happen by observing our fellow humans and being aware of our surroundings. On one particular occasion, I sat on the open decks outside the buffet café on board a magnificent ship. Quietly, I watched folks as they made their way from the swimming pool area, into the café at the rear of the ship. It was a walkway with tables on one side and a wall on the other. The path was not too wide and about sixty foot long. It was a great education for me as I observed my fellow passengers meander towards the enticing lunchtime food.

All types, shapes and sizes walked down the pathway to the food court. One lady, looked like a giant Super Nova waiting to explode. Four hundred pounds of sheer appetite eagerly swaggering towards the café, thinking about gobbling up the next few platefuls of food ... Perhaps was thinking ...

My appetite is my Shepherd, I shall not want,
It leadeth me into the path of temptation,
My belly floppeth over my knees,
Yay; though I walk through the valley of enticement, I will not weaken.
My taste buds are my rod, meat n' cream cakes comforteth me,
Though I dig my grave with my teeth, I shall fear no weight gain,
Later, after my lunch feast, I will snooze all afternoon, ready for the onslaught of
dinner n' midnight buffets ... with a few snacks in between,
After all, aren't we here to "enjoy" ourselves?

One of the dancers on board who was rushing to eat her yogurt and three lettuce leaves before her next rehearsal followed her. Isn't it amazing how the image of a human body can change shape so dramatically in just a few seconds? We are what we think and take shape with what we eat.

If we can control our thoughts, we can control our shape ... No fad diet can work for long ... There are no quick fixes... Training the taste buds to eat smaller potions in the best way to lose weight and keep it off.

Next came a couple of guys smoking cigars, talking about the stock market as they passed by. They were most upset that they were asked to put out their cigars before they entered the café. They came out with an insult in some foreign language and went back to the pool area where they were serving hot dogs, hamburgers and french fries.

Maybe we should bring smoking back into cafes, for isn't it unfair that folks can't smoke in restaurants and inflict their poisonous smoke on others? Alternatively, do you think it is best to ban smoking in all public areas?

We have stopped folks from smoking in many restaurants, airplanes and theaters. However, the medical profession is just beginning to realizing that negative thoughts are the most harmful toxins a human can consume.

The question now is, how can we stop folks from taking toxic thoughts into a cafe and digesting them?

I sat there for quite a while watching all the different people amble by and quite a few had one thing in common. None of them were smiling; they had very serious looks on their faces. The only really happy smiling faces I could see were those of the staff. The busboys and girls were very busy clearing the tables and they were the happiest. Joking and trying to make the passengers feel happy. A credit to the ambiance the ship was providing.

Many folks onboard seemed to be enmeshed in thoughts of past memories and the fact they were on a beautiful sailing resort did not mean anything.

The cruise industry does a great job of keeping folks happy with lots of shows and fun events. However, these moments of happiness are fleeting and all too soon, folks are taken back to worries and woes of past experiences. When the fun episodes are over, other images come into their minds. They could be back at work, or in a snowstorm. Locked in a dungeon of doom and gloom ... The looks on the faces of those shrouded in negativity were in-deed, grim and miserable.

My, oh my, why do people continue to live with negative minds?
Could it be we become addicted to worry?
An addiction is something we hate but can't get enough of.

There is a way through the maze of ignorance and into the light but most folks will not take that enchanting journey. Many call it mumbo jumbo and continue to live in a tormented mind. Amazing what a curse and bully the ego can be.

Once we plant seeds of worry in our minds, we encourage weeds of depression.

The best approach to rid the mind of destructive thoughts is to detach negative images from the brain. Dig them out with authentic reasoning. If we take pills or any other short-term measures to rid them, we are only cutting the stems off. The root cause of worry is still there. We need to spray our minds with universal love & joy emanating from deep within the heart and soul. The weeds of disquiet will dissolve away, replaced with a beautiful bouquet of flowering delights. These taste and feel real good and do not put on weight.

We need to find and understand the cause of our anxieties and not just treat the effects.

Just as I was, about to leave, a very feeble old man, walking with a cane, came struggling down the thoroughfare. He looked like a very old version of Mr. Grace from 'Are You Being Served' (an old British sit com) He looked as though he was one hundred and twenty years old. I found out later he was 'only' ninety-one. His mouth was wide open all the time. He reminded me of the bodies they dug up in Pompeii. He was very frail and every step seemed like his last.

When he finally made it to the doors of the café, he poked his head inside and a look of bewilderment came over him. He turned round and started to walk back towards the swimming pool. After a couple of minutes, he made the sixty foot walk back. Another look of amazement came over him. He stood there for a few moments gazing around contemplating his surroundings. He then turned round and started to make his backtrack way to the café. By this time everyone was looking at him. He leisurely made his way back to the café, mouth wide open, legs bowed, as thin as two sticks.

Once he got to the café, the doors opened again and again there was a look of wonderment on his face. He turned round and started to make his way back. As he passed my table, I was just about to ask if I could help him, when one of the servers came up to him and inquired `can I help you sir.' He stopped looked up at her and asked;

"Which way is it to the Gymnasium!"

Yes, I know it may not seem real ...but it really did happen.

A healthy appetite obeys a healthy diet, a fatty appetite emulates fatty foods.

SLICE FIFTEEN
Flushed With Success

For three months the toilet in the master bathroom decided to take a very slow twenty minutes to fill after a flush. Spraying with WD40 did not work, so finally an experience plumber was called in to remedy the situation. He took the top off the toilet cistern, scratched his crunch a few times whilst gazing at the green and yellow worn parts. He declared there was nothing he could do as the one piece system was twenty -five years old and the valves had all but ceased up. The only solution would be a whole new system. Not being one who accepts defeat so easily I ask if he was sure and was assured for certain the toilet was un-fixable. Still, it did not ring true, so I thanked him for his advice and sent him on his merry way.

As luck would have it, the next day my wife was playing golf with a new member of the club. She was a charming Irish lady from Montreal and she said her husband owned a large plumbing business. She is a snowbird who just happens to live in the same condo building. With 270 units it is virtually impossible to know everyone who lives in the building. When my wife returned home we talked about her new friend and thought it would do no harm to ask her husband if his toilet was working OK, considering it was the same as ours.

A few days went by and my wife rang her new best golfing buddy to make arrangements for their next game. On mentioning our problem toilet, the friend put her husband on the phone and before you could say Jack Robinson, he was in our bathroom looking at the cistern. He pulled out a monkey wrench. Turned two screws, pulled out a small plunger from the cistern and wiped a small piece of dirt from the tip. That's the culprit he declared ... Hey Presto! The toilet flushed better than ever and filled within fifteen seconds. It was as good as new. The whole problem was caused by a small piece of dirt that congested the whole system.

How many millions of dollars are spent each year on new appliances and systems because the so called experts do not know how to maintain good quality merchandise, so they contend the only solution is a new, (less well-made,) model. More to the point, how many people's minds are congested by a little piece of dirt from past events, which congests the whole mind and body during its lifetime?

When a person has to visit the doctor to repair an obstructed system, caused by impediments in the mind, the doctor treats the symptoms of the blockage without ever exploring what is causing the affliction. Medication extends to more, stronger medication, to alleviate symptoms cause by the original medication. Over time the wholes system packs in from lack of proper, proficient maintenance

Unfortunately, where the human body is concerned, the person cannot go out and buy a new model to replace the old one. If major surgery cannot fix-up the body, it expires without the true cause of congestion ever being discovered. Even when surgery is a successful outcome, the old blockage in the mind is seldom removed and the person still eventually dies with all the real riches of joy, left as good as new, switched off, in an inactive mode.

Dirt from past events is hard to remove if we do not possess the expertise to remove the congested part of the memory banks. Past thought that hold on to and replay revenge, anger, hatred, jealousy, anxiety and all other negative blockages over and over again. Obstructions that clog a conscious mind from living a happy, loving life. How easy it is to abandon hope of a truly joyful life when we cannot forgive past hurtful events and missed opportunities.

Settling for a mediocrity because professional expert dictate nothing can be done to change the situation other that prescription drugs is not the answer people require. They need to locate the genius that lives inside their mind and body that does know how to remove the blockages and clear the mind of regrets and disappointments.

It is a rekindling of the spark of authentic meaning that everyone embraces in their deep sub-consciousness. It is a knowingness that we really never own anything material that we can take with us on our eternal journey.

If we comprehend we do not actually own anything ... We understand we only rent a certain amount of space and time ... We can release all the congestion, to make room for a life of affectionate bliss with no attachments to negative thoughts ... We flush away all the sewerage that impeded our minds and can in-deed be regarded as a flushing success.

People who be-lie-ve they seriously know will never simply understand.

SLICE SIXTEEN
God's Business.

God is not for sale … However; many religious organizations believe they can extract money from people so that the people can pray to God … whilst they prey on the people. (Nah! Who would fall for that scheme other that people who have been indoctrinated with fear and guilt?) Religions should be "clubs" celebrating the joys of life together, in kindred spirit, at local meeting places. The celebration of life is dear to the hearts of all people of all race and creed. But, to use God as a means of inflicting fear and trepidation into innocent gullible people is nothing short of extortion beyond the laws of legislation.

Religion should be a social club that encourages folks to enjoy life by understanding the true make up of a human being. It should reveal the authentic nature of spirit that is the life force in "all things" (The Soul.) It should be a congregation of learning and creative arts...

It should not be a money making scam. It should be an assembly of sharing sameness, not a place of 'Higher-Archie' and elitism that divides society with hatred of other people because they do not conform to their male Gods falsehoods. And, if you don't follow teaching of certain religions their male God will humanely and mercifully make you burn in hell for eternity. ..Can you get more ignorant, primitive and uncivilized than that?

Even on the personal level, a few people believe they have a superior direct line to God (Spiritual guru's or masters) They believe people will pay them money to find out what God has told them and they have special intuitive powers to heal in some way. (Now that appears to be even more ludicrous, nobody would fall for that baloney...would they?) Every person has special powers to heal themselves and they need no guru or religion to teach them what they already know within their own true form. They only need to be aware of who they are and the reason they exist.

There are even more sinister dangers within the God Business. Many groups and organizations have sprung up, hiding behind a spiritual mask.

This cluster of ignorance contains left or right wing political groups and anarchists who wish to create their own particular brand of undemocratic lunacy.

Hitler's Nazi party started out as an occult spiritual party and the Swastika was a powerful emblem of the Sun. Hitler said; "the Christian God was for the weak and his God was for the strong." The rest of that story is history. The "spiritual" political groups of flakes and fakes of today are cut from the same mold as Hitler's occult and hatred of other humans is their motivation. They enroll innocent folks who have lost faith with mainstream religion and feel society has not treated them in a just manner. Out of ignorance of their true self, they get on the spiritual band wagon of cunning and conniving harebrained schemes that demand they should take control of society, so they can inflict their brand of unbalanced insanity. There business is a political God business. Their spiritual veil will conceal their intent, which is to wreak havoc on society with their inept, out of tune political doctrines.

Do you think God has become a very lucrative business that keeps a few people in luxury and power whilst their flocks live in poverty in many parts of our world?..... This does not mean that wealthy people and corporations should not support spiritual wisdom....In-deed it should be their first priority to do so........Well, just who is God and what type of business is he running?

What if God is not the creator of our universe? Before you go off at the deep end and say I am unsound, wait a moment. I did not say God does not exist, I said what if God did not create our universe. What if God has not got any control on what happens to earth, or to humanity. What if the folks who wrote the bible distorted the facts of creation! As we all know, rumors, superstitions and delusions do turn into folk laws. They can, and do turn into dogmatic belief systems.

- Over a long time span, different sections of humanity became entrenched into a belief system. Once any belief system is recognize as "normal" it become very difficult to remove it. There is no doubt the bible contains great wisdom and many stories have a metaphysical truth to them... However, past myths are not helpful to a specie of animals who embodies an intellectual flair for storytelling and inventiveness. In today's world we have many belief system and very little authentic meaning. The intelligence of God will never be fathomed by humanity......But perhaps these following facts are closer to the truth than the belief systems we live with at present?

- Creation is formed from elements of heat and cold combined with gases. It is infused with a life force of intelligence. All is created by an identification we refer to as Spirit, not God.

    God is a force of infinite intelligence far beyond the human minds capabilities of connecting to it. If we could access one fraction of Gods powerful dimension, for one split second, it would frazzle earth back into gasses. God is not directly approachable.

- God sets into motion the ingredients that contain all possibilities and permits the dice to fall where they land.

    A God genesis is an energy we specify as Spirit that contains infinite intelligence. Spirits energy manifests itself in a random manner within a unified framework of materialistic, temporal possibilities. All outcomes have already been planned out in multi-dimensional facets of pure potential.

- God has no jurisdiction on which way the materialistic forms will take shape. In other words, God presses the button (Releases Spirit) and starts the motor running and the results of the creation/evolution will become as random or as unified as the creation/evolver (Spirit) demands. These demands are explained by science as the outcomes of Quantum physic. In reality, control of events and happenings are dependent on each circumstance.

- God is the architect of Spirit, therefore it is the Spirit of God. Not God, who is the creator/evolver that manifests materialistic form that we designate as our universe... If we acknowledge Spirit is NOT God, rather Spirit is a random/united form of intelligence that can produce everything from nothing and visa versa ... then we will not any disputes over the identity of God within religion.

It is understood that the intelligence of God is far greater than anything humanity can absorb. Therefore; even if anyone does have a "good idea" of who God is, it would be too preposterous for them to relate that information at this time in human development, for it will only be guess work at best. And we cannot base our truths on guess work.

Let us change the wickets and play a new game. Here are the credible facts of God and Spirit that we can digest in our new game called...... "Keeping out of Gods Business."

- God is Not directly connected to the human race...Spirit is. Spirit has no distinct form and cannot be claimed to be "exclusively possessed" by any religion or science.
- God plays no part whatsoever in the way humanity develops...Spirit does and it can manifest itself into anything known and unknown. Humans are just one facet in a multi dimensional diamond.
- God is beyond all things human...Spirit is the only connection to creation/evolving
- God is beyond all things manifested into physical form...Spirit is connected all the *time*.
- God cannot be contacted by any human form....Spirit can be accessed all the *time.*
- God has an existence that cannot be fathomed by any intelligence source the universe provides. In other words, humanity is not privy to information that does not concern it!
- Spirit is an unemotional intelligence that constructs and destructs physical matter by random/unified choice. Humanity cannot change the will of Spirit. We are an element of spirit (souls)
- Spirit is akin to the weather...It can, and does change physical shape at a moments notice.
- Spirit is indestructible and we are all made from spirit...as are all life forms. All life is in spirits image in its true form. (without substance form)
- Spirit provides all of humanities requirement, no more, no less...we can ask for nothing!

Everything is provided! We need give no thanks to spirit...for it is self praise. In this new game praying to God is a complete waste of time and will not improve our life on earth. Listening to Spirit will improve our lifestyle and it is the only way humanity gains information to progress. We are already spirit (A soul) that can transform into "any-thing."

We have been given a human existence and an intellect that is fed by spiritual intelligence. It can construct and it can destruct. We can choose how we use this power. The closer we live to our true identity, the more creative we become. The more we distance ourselves from our true self, the more destructive we become. (Does this game make more sense than the game we are playing right now?)

In this game organized religions that preach man made dogmas are a complete sham and a waste of money and time. Once we allow God to get on with what he does, we can embrace spirit and no-body can divide spirit up and say this spirit is better than that spirit. It would be like saying, this blade of grass is better, than that blade of grass....we forfeit arguments about God in this new game.

Now let us backtrack into history a little.

The first monolithic religion was Judaism and anyone who has studied that religion will recognize the similarities to many stories in Greek mythology. One God religion was fashioned by one mans vision (Abraham) of a male God. His father was a very successful idol maker.

Abraham was brought up in the God business and decided he did not like the idols image (pardon the pun) We all know how many sons want to better their fathers ideas. So, Abe resolved to created a new image more in-keeping with his idea of a male, mythical, invisible God. (That's what comes of giving children a good education...They want to make changes, but not always for the better for many times they are half baked ideas)

But how was he to persuade he people to follow this male God? Also; Perhaps Abe's son said;

I want to go into Grandpa's business and sell idols when I grow up (typical little cheeky chap, just like his dad)So; dear Abe thought; Son...your messing with the wrong cowboy!

He came up with the idea that God has asked him to sacrifice his son and of course when it came to the moment of sacrifice God relented and said; Yay Verily "I was only testing your faith." (And teaching the brat-kid a lesson)

"Just kid-ding around Abe, now get me a goat to sacrifice" (pardon the pun) With Abraham being a very rich and influential man, the superstitious folks around him thought ... if it is good enough for him ... then we all want to be beholden to this male God who can punish us or treat us kindly. (And look how well mannered his son is now) What spectacular PR indeed.

And, as they say, the rest is history. Just what humanity needed.... A moody male God who has nothing better to do than play life and death games with backward, uninformed people.

I wish I could say they all lived Happy ever after!

It was all downhill after that. We could now kill people with a clear conscious and say "Our God tells us those people are infidels... so we had to murder them!" (This is being played out today by suicide bombers who are indoctrinated by their "holy men connected to God")This image of God is the root cause of millions upon millions of deaths throughout time. (How do you like this good old fashioned game of alienation).

Let's move on and grasp just one past example (within a multitude of abhorrence) of the flagrant atrocities within religion... About two thousand years ago Jewish Zealots of Judea murdered anyone who would not conform to their dogmatic belief systems. This is known as the first holocaust.

Whilst the Romans were on the outside of the walls of Jerusalem calling for surrender, the Zealots were on the inside murdering all the Jews who would not conform to their insane doctrines. Innocent people were torn between the devil and the deep blue sea (die at the hands of religious Zealots or heathen Romans) Six hundred, thousand people were slain and the male God said...All is Good?

A few years later rabbi Jesus came along and tried to change all the nonsense. Two hundred years later Christianity was formed based on reformed Judaism. Jesus' teaching, which by this time had probably been distorted out of shape, became written in stone as a power basis that would grow into the hundreds of segments it is today.

If Jesus could see how his philosophy has been so misrepresented, he would be utterly appalled. For sure, he would try again to turn the tables on all money and power seeking religious, dogmatic leaders... All religions have caused the deaths of millions of innocent people! Even within the myriads of each religion there is extensive disagreements and hatreds of their own divided segments. This is the insanity we live with today.

It seems:

The more religious a person becomes ... the more dogmatic they become.

The more the dogmatic behavior ... the further fundamentalism stretches.

The more the fundamentalism reaches ... the more power to the leaders ...The more power to the leaders ... The bigger the wars, mayhem and terrorism.

Nearly all wars are based on some form of belief system and humanity has got their existence all messed up and tangled in a web of deceit and lies. That is why humanity has to keep killing each group or tribe that comes along with a different belief system. For each fabricated system will reveal the futility of the other system that wishes to obliterate them.

There is NO possible way of living in peace with the present belief systems humanity is entrapped into. The problem is compounded by the fact that all religions do contain some components of spirits truth.

There is a blueprint within the soundness of Spirit that can guide humanity to prosper and enjoy its existence on earth. Many wise sages have touched spirits mind and much wisdom has been derived....But that wisdom has been abused, misused and exploited by unscrupulous humans who wish to exert power over the masses. Religion does not have the answers to humanities problems; on the contrary, it magnifies them.

Likewise science does not possess too many of the answers to aid humanity to live an authentic life. If science is undertaking to read the mind of God they will need to find some other method than mathematics, for God lives outside any essence that correlates with the human mind.

But what if God could talk to us, what would he say? Well, let's do a little experiment and imagine we can hear God speak to us...

As God almighty, in multi-dimensional guises of intelligent energy, I am everyone's friend on earth, but most people no longer recognize me as their friend, so I guess I am not so mighty? ... Well, that is because it is not my intent to make anyone do what he or she does not want to do.

From my experience, I can honestly say as an omnipresent, universal, evolving/creating God, that I have never lost a friend; however, many friends have lost my company ... more so in the last few thousand years, as I silently talk more freely about the genuine way to live life on earth.

I understand many of my earthly, human friends have their quirks and idiosyncrasies and I have learnt to play along with their perspectives whilst speaking universal, indisputable truth. I speak in silent tones directed at the intelligence of human intuition, insights, feelings, etc...All outside the intellects/egos grasp, however not outside its reach and understanding.

Unfortunately, because of human's religious beliefs, superior education, scientific knowledge or social standing, they perceive my simplicity is not to their sophisticated liking and their opinions can no longer associate themselves with me as their God without any labels.

I am the first to admit my cup of simplicity runneth over and in the eyes of sophisticated people, who consider themselves to be clever in some way or other, that just will not fit into the image of who they be-lie-ve themselves to be... That is why they have vanquished themselves from my paradise.

Maybe they be-lie-ve their religious doctrine is sacrosanct and no other viewpoint can be tolerated?

Maybe they be-lie-ve their social embellishes are paramount and anyone who cannot conform will not be stomached?

Maybe they be-lie-ve science and technology can replace me with man-made theories.

Whatever the reason, I have found people with a simple smile and a non- involvement in normal social gossip, or one sided viewpoints, such as politics and world events with an authoritarian left or right slant, will not be tolerated.

Thankfully, I still have a few good friends who listen in silence to me and do not live in shallow minds. They beam my smile at birth and a few carry it with them throughout their lives.

On the surface many people seem like they are not bothered by fresh, invigorating, inspirational viewpoints, however when that viewpoint contains authentic universal truths, intellectual/ egotistical people will run miles away and for sure, keep their distance.

It seems if I, the only authentic, cosmic power in the universe, cannot fit in with a social tribal mentality, then I will be condemned to isolation by that group and replaced with a man-made ideology. Funny thing is, some of the religious groups are theoretically textbook spiritual, however, I find their theology cannot be lived in a joy-filled mind... As if, their doctrine and dogma, can replace my love and joy.

Others are motivational life coaches, professors, or other professional experts who want to train their pupils to become catch-phrase-parrots so that they can find their pot of gold... As if, money and possessions can replace me?

Some are psychologists or medical groups who want to put band-aids on symptoms rather than curing the causes. ...As if, humans can repair a body and mind better than I can?

Yes in-deed, if I do not conform to people's be-lie-fs and keep my happy, silent mouth shut, I cannot be accepted in any circle of society that wants it to be their way or the highway. In every case, my high-way is the conductor of life's enchanting orchestrations

The laughable thing is I have never fallen out with anyone in my life and only desire the best of every-thing, for every-body.

Because human time passes by so fast, I would like to remind you that I continue to send blessings in the direction of all my friends on earth who are open to receive them. I abide in an infinite house, filled with harmony and peace and send everyone love and joy from my eternal heart and ageless soul.

Always remember, Idols need to be broken before God can appear!

SLICE SEVENTEEN
Questions and Answers from a Professional Optimist

1. Q: In a world that seems so full of despair, or as the Buddhist puts it, when all life is suffering, is it possible to maintain a healthy and Optimistic world view?

A: Suffering is a state of mind that holds tommyrot ... Why live in a garbage bin? Intellectual opinionated convictions beam as the truth erodes. The most reliable technique to demolish the truth is to intellectualize it and then market it to the masses as disciplined, authentic facts. Allow the heavens and stars to praise your ability to become nothing in a comfortable state of mindlessness. From this location God exists as your partner and you dance together as one spirit inside the rhythm of the cosmos.

2. Q: How is it possible to maintain an optimistic world view in the face of Reality, i.e., global warming, inevitability of death, war, etc.?

A: Throughout a person's lifetime, the truth awaits in silences for wisdom to prevail. Somewhere along on the way, beliefs lead to interpretations ... Interpretations lead to opinions ... Opinions lead to conflicts ... Conflict leads to death. Physical death is inescapable and world events continue to project disasters, however eternal energy cannot disappear, cannot burn and cannot drown ... Why fear death & disasters when the immorality of the essence of a human being feels so much better. More often than not belief and faith resist the truth.

3. Q: How do you keep a positive outlook during major life setbacks? For example: A loved one who has been in a major car accident, your honor roll teenager who has taken a turn on the wrong path, a young mother/father who is dealing with a child in their terrible two's, a person dealing with vindictive in-laws, or one who has been fired from a job with no income to pay the bills?

A: The true identity of a human being does not see life as a duality of positives and negatives. Only the ego views life's events on an emotional roller coaster. Everyone will experience things that hold the potential to set their negative emotions alight. When their wisdom intervenes and they view the negative emotions as finite illusions joy becomes unavoidable. Bottom line -To make life simple, look for possible problems before they occur and then work out possible solutions.

4. Q: A skeptic might ask if an eternal optimist is simply delusional. How would you respond?

A: People who compare themselves to other people live a mediocre existence. Not only skeptics will view my philosophy as stupid, most clever people will also view them as delusional and I have to say I agree with them most wholeheartedly. In the eye's of people who consider themselves clever I will always be stupid and I am happy with that. A wasp on an outside window cannot sting you.

5. Q: Can you recommend positive thinking exercises that one may use to guard themselves from pessimists and negative thoughts. When negative influences do nothing but make you self-doubt your inner strengths, what can you do?

A: There is no way to avoid positive or negative thoughts if a person is the participant in any event in their lives. By living with an objective detachment, as a witness rather than the participant a person can avoid negative thoughts. The truth is surrounded by everyone else's point of view. The mind and body cells function on original intelligence systems that differ from the thoughts transmitted from the thinking brain. The mind/body cells indulges the intellect that can oppose its intelligence a little, however, if the discord continues for any lengthy period, the naturally happy mind/body cells are not amused. The best way, to get your own way, is to learn to be happy anyway.

6. Q: How do people stay positive in a society that is increasingly Superficial?

A: Enjoy all the superficial stuff as long as the ego is the servant and not the master.

Big Ego = Big Fall

Little Ego = Little Fall

Joyful Ego = Joy-F-All

Positive Ego = Enjoy God's Order

Negative Ego = Ease God Out

Bottom Line ... Try not to fake yourself too seriously

7. Q: Does optimism usually tie into religion or philosophy or is it simply a personal attitude?

A: Any doctrine that raises the fear threshold has a negative value. No human intellectual understanding can talk truth; therefore personal views are very limiting. A connection to universal intelligence feeds the mind all the things it needs to live a prosperous life on earth...who can ask for more. Bright lights shine brightest in dark shadows.

8. Q: Depression characterizes--and is often the result of--a chemical imbalance. Couldn't a habitually optimistic outlook be viewed within the same biochemical framework? If so, what are the implications?

A: A human brain and body function by chemical balance amongst other effects. It is the thoughts, fed by or starved of universal spirit that regulates the scales of balance. Life is permeated with riddles. Some are small, some are large, and some are sent as half riddles. Every riddle requires understanding before they can be solved. If we only have half the riddle we need to explore where the other half exists and what the whole riddle means... Then and only then will we find true answers. I never try to challenge truth ... But I am delighted to live by it. Inasmuch as my heart, lungs, other organs, trillions of cells, particles and molecules communicate to me what they desire. I then try to understand the subconscious part of my brain that is connected to this vast reservoir of intelligence and allow the conscious part of my brain to fill the requirements.

9. In what ways do negative thoughts affect a person? What effects do positive thoughts have on a human being?

All positive and negative thoughts have a cause and effect on a person's health, wealth and happiness. So, when a person eliminates positive and negative thought all will become divine. The universe supplies everyone with a treasure chest of unprocessed energy by way of creative thoughts ... How they refine them accommodates the harvests or the famines in their life. Always remember ... People who put both feet in one trouser leg shuffle through life!

Everything carved in the halls of time erodes on the breeze of eternity.

SLICE EIGHTEEN
Why Unethical Companies Continue To Thrive

One of the strange quirks in the modern world is the fact that most unethical companies thrive, while many companies that try to preserve the environment and people's health struggle to survive.

The laws of supply and demand will invariably be the ultimate reason why any business succeeds or fails. Moral ethics do play a major role eventually; however, it may take many years before any moral ethics play out their role in the demise of unsavory companies.

When flawed habits of consumers support a business, it will permit a company, with low moral ethics/products to thrive. Foods that contain trans-fats and other harmful substances to a persons health are consumed on a daily basis by millions of people.

Why do people eat and smoke if they know it is bad for their health? Well, I guess people will say they want to live as they wish to live therefore, as long as people demand cigarettes, tobacco companies will be profitable and the air polluted in the vicinity of smokers.

Tobacco company directors know cigarettes can kill people who smoke, but they feel their obligation is to make a profit for the shareholders and supply the demand of the consumer. Therefore, we can only have ethical companies when people understand the true meaning of moral ethics of their own mind and body.

The greed and ignorance of companies who sell harmful products only reflects the greed and ignorance of the people who run them, which in turn, reflects the people within the society they live who demand the products.

In a nutshell ... People need to learn why they could become addicted to harmful habits and then resist the habit before it can take hold. Whether it be; junk food, alcoholic drinks, prescription drugs, tobacco products or any other product that can harm human life. For people who are already addicted, breaking harmful habits can only come about by an overhaul of a person's mis-conditioned mind. Living with moral ethics towards ones own body and mind requires far-reaching changes in the way society perceives living an authentic life on earth.

Consequently, getting rid of unethical companies will take a large number of people with harmful habits to change their way of life. It will also require many wise educators to teach the young of today, to challenge any thoughts they may have of becoming addicted to harmful habits.

The old adage; treat others in the same way we would like to be treated, can only hold true, when we treat our own minds and bodies with the respect they deserves.

When people do stop buying products detrimental to their health, it will send unsavory companies into bankruptcy.

I am sure there are many human egos who will disagree with this chain of thought; accordingly, sorry to say, unethical companies are a possible investment for eager investors, for the foreseeable future.

A good education, hard work and luck account for 10% of our prosperity...The balance comes from somewhere else, thus most live in ignorance of true Points of Life!

SLICE NINETEEN
The Wisdom of the S-ages

Why do people have such difficulty in maintaining a steady weight throughout their lives? Many people buy books on the latest trendy diets only to find short-lived success in finding the contented weight balance.

Don't dig your grave with your own knife and fork. ~*English Proverb*

It seems no amount of counseling or advice can solve the problems permanently. Therefore, what are the techniques to maintain a sensible weight?

- A good diet of wholesome foods, whole grains, fruit and vegetables will help reduce unsound cravings.
- Extra antioxidants will aid the body to overcome nutrition depleted foods.
- Regular exercise will improve overall health.
- Sleeping soundly throughout the night will provide clearer thoughts.
- Drinking at least six glasses of water a day will help reduce taste bud desires.
- Deep breathing at selected points of the day will lessen tension
- Massage will lend a helping hand to reduce false hunger pangs.
- Meditation will quiet the mind and settle the appetite for a short time.
- Doing charitable work will take the focus off eating for a while.

One should eat to live, not live to eat. ~*Cicero*

However, none of the above will be a lasting solution to an ongoing basis for reoccurring overeating issues. It is low self worth, which stems from daily erroneous events, that causes people to seek comfort foods containing too much sugar and fat, which pile on the pounds.

People's natures are alike; it is their habits that separate them. ~*Confucius*

There is only one ageless answer, which will prove to be a sure _ fired success in finding a permanent solution to weight control.

A complete overhaul of self_ identification is required before any person can truly bring about a change in overall well-being and happiness.

To lengthen your life, shorten your meals. ~*Proverb*

A contented mind is a happy mind. It can only be contented if it is free from thoughts and memories installed by other people's beliefs and opinions from early childhood. If the reference points in the mind are continually playing themes that induce fear, hatred, and worry, then no external aid will take that away. Only if a person realizes negative emotions are the ego's illusions, can they tear themselves away from their persistent afflictions. To know thyself is to find true self-worth.

It is one's own mind, not enemies, that lures evil ways. ~*Buddha*

Every cell, molecule and atom of a human being is filled with intelligent energy that conveys serene tranquility. However, when the mind is fed erroneous negative thoughts from a false self-image, the conscious mind believes it requires tasty, unhealthy foods to soothe the uneasiness. This becomes a constant, self-fulfilling habit. In the empty nothingness of every cell exists the dance of primary life that organizes a wholesome being. This intelligent energy force is the true identity of every person on earth. Many times, it is overpowered by the demands of the ego/ personality.

Clogged with yesterday's excess, the body drags the mind down with it. ~*Horace*

When we tune into the nothingness of each cell we can rejoice with their intrinsic delight. When this realization passes through from our subconscious, into our conscious mind, it is impossible to feel anything other than authentic contentment of self worth, no matter what external circumstances are playing out their illusionary role-play. Changing the concept of who we believe we are, is the only way to dissolve the habit of overeating the wrong foods and preserving a healthy stabilized body and mind.

When we strip our mind down to the bare essentials we find the naked truth.

Slice Twenty
The Quest for Paradise on Earth

A time ago upon once, a brave knight, dressed in the best of glittering armor, rode proudly through the countryside seeking good deeds to perform. One day he happened upon a sight never seen before. A large neon sign "Paradise" shone over a de-light-ful place filled with hues in tones of superb eloquence. He laughed out loud and wondered who erected such a nonsense sign, for he knew there was no such place as paradise on earth.

As he approached on horseback the road suddenly turned to gold. He could see the gates to the entrance of Paradise ahead. Being the most brave and courageous knight in the land, he decided to make a grand entrance and find the joker who built this mirage. Smacking his horse, he galloped as fast as he could towards the entrance. All at once he hit an invisible bubble that covered Paradise and was thrown from his horse.

As he picked himself up with disheveled pride he could see his horse trotting though the gates with no trouble at all. Thinking he may have fallen off the horse he ran headlong into the invisible bubble once more. This angered him more than ever, so in a great rage, he pulled out his sword and gave the invisible bubble a mighty whack. The sword shattered into a thousand pieces and the handle melted in his hand. He realized all at once that this in-deed was the true place of paradise.

As he contemplated what to do next, a little boy appeared on the other side of the invisible bubble eating a peanut and banana sandwich on whole-wheat toasted bread. The little boy chuckled and softly said, "You cannot enter here with armor, you must first remove it before you gain entrance." Since he had nothing on under the armor he was hesitant to remove it; however, with his curiosity now aroused, he stripped off all the armor and leisurely tried to walk though the invisible bubble.

He now felt dejected and downhearted and asked the youngster why he could not enter. He stated he had always done good deeds to help people in distress. Also, he was the cleverest knight in all the land, having scribed many papers on mathematics, science and the arts.

The little boy sniggered kindly and while still munching on his delicious sandwich declared, "You don't understand; the armor you need to remove is not on the surface of your body, it is in your mind. You have filled your brain with all the knowledge and education that your ego, personality and intellect hangs onto as their realities. You have imprisoned your thought process with cleverness and pride of who you be-lie-ve yourself to be.

"Even though you are doing good deeds and are a truly brave and courageous knight, you have evicted yourself from Paradise by your own cleverness that lives outside the realms of truth. On one side of your brain, the subconscious lives in emptiness filled with wisdom. On the other side of your brain the conscious — ego/intellect, personality — lives with all types of labels and role plays — all filled with taxing, trying, weighty demands, diffi-cult ideas, and laborious perceptions. It rides in rough terrain of negative emotions, all of which are illusionary as they do not exist in Paradise.

"It is the simple mind of tranquility and serenity that can guide the mind to use its thoughts in love and joy, which allows all its deeds and actions into Paradise. When you can detach your mind-set from the incarceration of your ego/intellect, the invisible bubble will evaporate into thin air.... It was never here in the first place and is not here now. You are the only one who constructed it and as you stand here in your nakedness outside the compass of Paradise, you need to ask yourself if it is time to become a knight of meek simplicity." With that, the little boy disappeared and the knight was left sitting on his horse gazing up at the starlit sky. As he stroked the horse's neck, little traces of peanut butter became visible on his fingers.

Tomorrow's memories are formulating from night- time's rainbow dreams.

SLICE TWENTY ONE
School Day Pranks.

Tom is a hundred years young today. To his delight, family and friends have made him a surprise birthday party. Everyone is sat at the large table when suddenly, great grandson Bobby, nine years of age, stands-up and asked him... What is the secret to living a happy, healthy life and still being active like you grandpa?

How do you keep so cheery and youthful at a hundred years of age?

Well Bobby, I have never grown up and become a staid and somber man like many other people I knew. I have never looked at life as serious-minded hurdles that needed to be tackled. I still love playing games and tricks on folks who take life far too seriously. Let me tell you a tale when I was your age...

I remember, as a cheeky kid of nine years of age, reluctantly attending school. I was full of simple mischief and fun. Nothing in comparison to what children do today with drugs and the like. Nonetheless, it still got me in hot water with my teachers, but I would always own up to any impishness I caused.

This meant I spent many happy hours outside the headmasters study waiting for his sadistic punishment. He was a beetroot faced character, permeated with the wrong kind of mean spirit......Whisky, I suspected by his breath, but what does a nine year old kid know?

In those days (1910) we would receive a leather strap smacked against our hand or backside, six times. They called it 'Six of the best.' It stung for a few minutes, but I always went out singing a nice tune, whilst the headmaster fumed with exasperation.

I remember one instance, it was the start of a new term and we had the pleasure of a young, fresh teacher, who the class regarded as an idiot savant ... Nicknamed, Dopey, to us kids. It was a golden opportunity for me. Every lesson, he struggled to teach English to a class of nine year olds, who preferred to be outside playing games in the playground.

One day, early in the morning lesson, I asked him if I could go see the doctor as I felt an affliction coming on. Without question, he agreed and as quick as Jack Flash, I ran out of school. There was a great circus and fun fair that just came into town and I wanted to enjoy the opening, free afternoon show.

As I was always honest, I did go down to the doctor's office, which just happened to be around the corner to the circus. I waited in the doctor's surgery (No appointment needed those days.) He called me into his office. I informed him "I've discovered two bumps on my head behind my left and right ears." After a careful examination he laughed at me. He was a good natured man and liked my sense of humor.

He declared, "You are fooling around aren't you. Those bumps have always been there, everyone has them. You are a cheeky little juvenile. Go home and bandage your head with vinegar and brown paper and keep it on for a month, without that saucy smile" he laughed teasingly. Well, I had the day off school and on the way to the circus; a new scheme was hatching in my cheeky mind.

The next day I came to school with my head bandaged-up and a very serious look on my face. Everyone was taken back for they have never seen my face looking distressful. I told the teacher "What I have requires careful, cautious treatment, so I need to sit at the back of the class and not be involved with any work." He asked me; "What have you got" and I replied; "The doctor said I must not smile for one whole month. The least that people know about my affliction, the quicker my bandages will come off. After the month is out, I will tell everyone about my affliction." He seemed a little puzzled, but replied "OK, you can tell me what affliction you have next month."

Well, for one whole month I sat at the back of the class and read my comic books with a sedated look on my face. I didn't do any homework and got off gym class. It was a month of pure unsophisticated loafing around. For a nine year old with no interest in school ... Paradise!

I could not get into trouble for playing truant and had the teachers blessing to do nothing but relax and read comic book stories. Money could not buy such cheer for a nine year old youngster ... Not that I had any money, apart from two pennies each week, to buy my comics, and a bag of candy.

When you play tricks there always come a day of reckoning and when the month was up the teacher called me out to the front of the class. With the head master by his side, to hear my explanation, he demanded an answer... "Now then" he said in a stern voice, trying to impress the headmaster who was looking grimmer than ever. "Tell us all what affliction you have been suffering."

As quick as a flash I whipped off the bandages, jumped up on the desk and shouted out-loud....

"I have been afflicted with... CHUTZPAH!"

The class roared with laughter and to my surprise so did the headmaster and the teacher. I think they were glad to see me smile again. It did not stop the headmaster from giving me a hard clip around the ear and I almost needed the bandages.

I am still a cheeky kid and I still have not lost the wisdom of a child who understood... Life is far too short to be taken seriously. Even when we are made to do things we don't care for ... we can still make it fun!

Ships (minds) that sail in calm (Love & Joy) waters savor a tranquil, divine life. Ships that sail in rough seas (negative emotions) live a worrisome, tumultuous life.

SLICE TWENTY TWO
Surrogate Joy

In recent years, scientific medical studies have concentrated their focus on the effects of a joyful mind. The aim is to determine if blissfulness can maintain a person's good health and wellbeing. The studies are disclosing what wise sages have known for centuries ...That a joy-filled mind will strengthen the immune systems resilience regards disease and supply all-over good health.

Even with all the new medical and spiritual information, people are less happy than previous generations. It seems the more affluent people become, the more misery they have to endure. Maybe many people surrender their joy in the expectation other people will return it to them.

- Do you live your life waiting for other people to lift your spirits?
- Are you dependant on shopping for luxury items to give you a quick fix of satisfaction?
- Do you need to be part of a social-set before you feel fulfilled in your personal self - esteem?
- Can you sit silently alone in a room, without reading a book, watching TV, talking to a friend or family member?
- Are you content and serene inside your own skin?

Many psychologists assert human beings are social animals and can develop depression if they are not part of a social group. As with most modern psychotherapy I read, I differ in my approach in overcoming the emotions of depression and unhappiness.

"You breathe all the time you're sleep, but you aren't living. I mean living ‒ doing the things you want to do . . . . That's what I call living, Aunt Polly. Just breathing isn't living!" _Pollyanna

Being part of a social group can make demands on a person's naturalness and many times will alter their simplicity into a more unnatural sophistication.

Humanity has neatly packaged itself into different groups, tribes, religions, cultures and traditions. Most people have no choice in their conformity, because, by the time they reached seven years of age, the die-has-been-cast and their reference points established.

However, once people mature and become fully fledged members of their clans, many inner feelings of dissent and discord can fester in the subconscious mind. These uneasy feelings can last a lifetime, but the person is powerless to break away for fear of retribution from the other clan members, who are mostly sensing the same uncomfortable pressures. Traditional habits are the most difficult to overcome, even though they may be pointless.

*"What men and women need is encouragement. . . . Instead of always harping on a man's faults, tell him of his virtues. Try to pull him out of his rut of bad habits."*_ Pollyanna

Before I go any further, I am not advocating you should become a hermit. Rather, I am contending it may not be a good idea to allow your joy to be dependant on any outside forces. To segregate your happiness by a reliance on any other person actions and emotions is to give up the powers of the joy you inherited at birth.

Here is a small sample list of the many ways you may be segregating your joy to other people in the hopes they will return the joy with interest.

1. Are you reliant on your child's success as a substitute for what you believe to be the failures in your own life's ambitions?
2. Do you live your life through the pages of the fashion magazines always needing to keep up with the latest trends to feel worthy?
3. Are you trying to imitate your favorite film, TV or pop star, whilst longing for their fame and fortune?
4. Do you need an award or certificate to convey you are a success?
5. Are you dependent on a compliment to give you an air of self-value?
6. Do the perceptions in your faith, ideas within your spirituality or theories in your non-beliefs, contain any attached elements of fear or anxiety?
7. Are your digested, conditioned thought principles, bringing all the rewards you should expect from then ... i.e. health, wealth, comfort and happiness? If not, what useful purpose do they serve, if their

performance is redundant and cannot relieve the stress of modern day living.

Throughout your life, significant circumstances will continually change for better or worse. However, the one real feeling that should grow moment by moment is your sense of joy. That can only be accomplished by a true sense of self... of who you are, and your rightful place on earth.

You belong right where you are located at any given moment in time, for you are an outgrowth of universal love that has evolved and created all you see, smell, touch, see and hear. During your lifetime, your bliss is your immortal treasure that conveys wellbeing and prosperity.

Beyond all your role-plays, you are an infinite bundle of joy packaged in a human body and mind that wants to explore all things material and tangible, whilst at the same time recognizing the identity of non-tangible blissfulness. Without this recognition, life will become meaningless and the search for happiness becomes a trivial pursuit that has no real rewards.

*"Hold up to him his better self, his real self that can dare and do and win out . . . People radiate what is in their minds and in their hearts."*_ Pollyanna

You cannot give your bliss away; you can only conceal it from your mind with the aid of your egos perceptions. So, enjoy your family, friendships, clans, religions, spirituality and culture, but never depend on any for your authentic joy...Your joy is who you are, within every cell and molecule of your being.

Be at-ease with the wisdom of knowing it is time to stop playing hide and seek with your happiness. It can never leave you without your permission to hide and now you know it has nowhere to run.

Do other people expect you to be serious and are you living up to their expectations?

SLICE TWENTY THREE
Gods Sorry, He's Made a Few Mistakes and Will Make Amends Soon.

I awoke one morning from a pleasant nights sleep and before my eyes focused clearly, the phone rang. The caller ID only read, celestial being, so I was not going to answer it. Well, you never know if it is the devil on the phone or God. I was in no mood to be talking to the devil so early in the morning, but when it comes to God, he can call at any time and I'm ready to listen to what he has to say, even though he complains all the time these days that nobody listens to him anymore.

I took a chance, it was God on the phone, and he was in an extra state of uneasiness. He told me he has been keeping a close eye on human behavior patterns the past few thousand years and realizes he has made a few mistakes when it came to the human body. We should note that one of Gods days equals ten thousand of our human years, so after closer observations of moral beings for a day, he has drawn up a new blueprint for the human race, because he sees the current model will be extinct before his next day is over. Here are a few of the novel designs God told me he is going to incorporate in the new human model, for he wants to make sure ... All is really good next time around.

The first change will be people will have a chimney on the top of their heads. The roof of the mouth will have a flap and when a person lights up a cigarette, the flap will automatically open and the smoke will go up a specially lined flue and will be filtered into clean air by the time it comes out the chimney. This will stop the smoke going into the lungs and causing people to die of lung cancer. He will also flavor the extracted clean air with lavender and frankincense so all non-smokers will invite smokers into their homes and enjoy their clean, mountain air tonic.

The next great idea God has come up with is to take out the liver, kidneys and bladder, replacing them with a distillery. No matter if a person drinks pure water, soda, beer, or spirits. It will pass through the body and into an express distillery. There will be a choice of many exotic alcoholic cocktails. Whatever a person thinks up will be transmitted by neurons to the distilleries mechanism, so that when the person urinates, they will pee into a glass and hay presto, they have their drink of the day. If they want to put a bit of fizz into the drink, all they need to do is jump on the spot for a minute and it will come out shaken, not stirred ... Self - replenishing drinks ... How cool is that!

The next measure he has implemented is to take out the intestines and digestive tract. This will be replaced with a fast food processing plant. Burgers, hot dogs, etc., will all be available on demand by just thinking about it. People will be able to eat whatever they want and just think what they would like for t he next meal. Then, before they can say Jack Robinson, the eaten food will be processed so that they can have an elimination and out will pop burgers and hot dogs, just the way they like them cooked. Of course, they will have to take a plate with them to the toilet, or they will have to fish out soggy burgers.

Yummy, I can just see your mouth watering at the thought of it.

There will be no requirement for doctors or pharmaceutical drugs, because in the new human model nobody will ever become sick or die of old age. The new structure will be made of flame and rust proof indestructible molecules, sinews and tissues, so people can abuse themselves from morning until night with smoking, drinking and overeating junk food and nothing will harm them.

However, God still likes his little jokes, so for the time being, he will keep the mind just the way it is now. People will still believe they have free will and can make up as many religions as they deem necessary, so that they can keep the flames of hatred burning brightly. In fact, hatred will be the main subject in all schools and made compulsory for every student. Science and intelligent design will be removed from the curriculum, for with hatred as the main subject, people will have plenty to fight over.

Society will still be able to wage destructive wars, only problem being, they will not be able to kill one another. They can invent all kinds of nuclear weapons, smart bombs, etc., but they will only be able to blow up buildings, animals, plants and trees. People will be indestructible, so they can create mayhem and chaos all the time, therefore, no need of video games or reality TV shows.

The fun has only just begun for God, for he will give each person a different language to speak, so nobody will be able to understand what anybody else is saying. It is not that much different from what we have now, with people who speak the same language and divide each other up into different groups, only this time around, the groups will only contain one person. Each person will be given the same name, but with a different model number. They will all be named, Frankenstein and each will have their own serial number.

Not all the new changes will be so much different to the medical professions present day model, which has altered the human body by removing intestines, face-lifts that go higher and higher with each season and all the other great gifts they have augmented. Its just that God has taken it to a more advanced level of sophistication and realizes it is what people are asking for each day.

God believes the fresh benefits are huge for his chosen races that are built in his image. Humans will be able to cut down all the trees once they can manufacture their own clean oxygen supply through their personal chimneys. If they run out of space, they can drain the oceans, because they have their own inner, ever regenerating, drinks machine ... Who needs water?

Once they run out of that space, they can build mega-homes of one million sq. feet. Impoverished people can sleep standing up and every human will own one sq. foot, in a million sq. foot home. Every common person can brag about living in a million sq. foot home. But not the rich people, they will have their own underground bunkers with all the modern day trappings of real wealth (but that's another story) Also, since they cannot kill each other and will live forever, they can breed animals, to kill them just for sporting fun in a new game called, animal wars. When they wipe all the game animals out, they can bomb the breeding factories and make animals extinct creatures.

Before too long, without any water, all the plants and flowers will perish and the earth will become a barren landscape ... A barren wasteland, which will resemble the moon, mars and all the other planets in our solar system. The good news is, it will save billions of dollars on future space missions, for who needs to visit barren planets when we will have contrived our own right here on earth. Yes indeed, home is where the heart is and a barren wilderness is a worthy home for aggressive humans. Indeed, God know, all will be better than good.

Of course, human beings have a great imagination and now they know Gods future plans they may beat him to it and restructure earth and the human body themselves. They may even concoct a completely new form of God and make this present-day one redundant. Perhaps they will devise a God that will remove the human brain, replace it with one that delights in greed, and fear more than the present model. The newfangled God can dispose of any feelings of love & joy, so that people can feel contented, soaking up other people's misery. Powerful, clandestine speculators will be able to manipulate the commodity markets more than they do now and make crude oil $1000 a barrel, Gold $10,000 an ounce, etc. Business can learn better ways to swindle people and cheating contests will be held for executives, who will get billion dollar bonuses for being the biggest swindlers.

Most people will remain poor, but with a chimney in their heads and a distillery in their tummies, who will care. Yes, future generations will have a lot to be thankful. They will be able to debate why life is so boring, whilst reminiscing about the good old days, when people could actually kill each other in wars,. Since they all talk different languages it will bring new life to the phrase "Actions speak louder than words"

So, let's raise our glasses and drink a toast to future prospects ... "Here's looking at you future generations, with the scheming red in your eyes and the venomous perversions in your grin."

I awoke in a pool of sweat realizing I had only been dreaming. I fetched the newspaper in from the front porch and read the headlines. I cried out ... Oh My God ... It was not a dream; he's begun to generate the changes!

A negative emotion is the fifth ace up the sleeve that cheats the holder out of a prosperous life.

SLICE TWENTY FOUR
The Meddling Neighbor Within.

When we were children, our mothers were busy cleaning the house, shopping, maybe going out to work to supplement the income. Many fathers were engrossed with their job. They may have been absent for long periods, so they never got much time to spend with their family.

Other fathers went down to the pub at night or had a game of cards arranged or other events with "the Boys." Some parents were only interested in their own social life, keeping up with the "Jones's" and a great many children felt neglected. There are many parents who abused their children and such actions at an early stage of life can be catastrophic. However, let's consider the effects of what most people will regard as a normal upbringing.

If we were the first baby of the family, we received a lot of attention but if other children came along, our younger brothers and sisters received the attention that we were getting. Unless our parents were very wise, pangs of jealousy began to fester If we became sick or had an accident, then all of a sudden the attention reverted back to us. As we advanced from toddler to infant, many actions and events we had no choice in, were deposited into our subconscious memory banks.

We have all encountered different experiences while we were maturing and these experiences will make us act and respond to the actions of the world in which we now live. Before we had reached the age of seven, many of us had been programmed with a multitude of negative thoughts. We had no choice in the matter. We had to conform to society doctrines and the teachings of other misguided people. Our ego's developed amidst a mass of negativity and we learnt that worry and anxieties are the normal way to respond to most of life's eventualities.

As we grew and ripened into adults, the conditioning from childhood taught us that to gain attention we must somehow or other project ourselves as being inadequate or sickly. Being very clever creatures of habit, the human mind will find subtle ways that are not obvious to project our ill health or inadequacies.

We started to realize that our family and friends are ignoring us so we become emotional, neurotic, angry and sometimes violent. We may go in the other direction and sink into our shells. We become withdrawn and unfriendly and feel we are a doormat for the world to tread on. We start to get in the habit of becoming a smoker, a drinker, an overeater, a user of social drugs and all these attachments become addictions we hate but can't get enough of them. We shelter behind our addiction so that the world will sympathize and pick on someone else to vent their displeasure of the life they are also living. We gather in groups of drinkers and this becomes a social event. Cocktails at seven sounds so cool but the cocktails are killing our brain cells and pickling our livers.

We overeat when we become stressed with our job, with our home life, our relatives and friends. We even become stressed as we age and look in the mirror to see a new wrinkle or gray hair. Even worse: no hair!! The cycle continues and the more we think of our inadequacies, the more stressed we become. We develop a sickness out of our dis-ease and run to the doctor for attention. As most of the doctors are sick themselves, they can only give medication that will alleviate the symptoms but cannot cure the stress. Would we ask a blind man for directions?

Some folks even brag about how many operations they have undergone. They did not get sick on purpose but past conditioning in their subconscious led them on a path of destruction for many years. All those years of anguish and torment, playing havoc with their immune systems. They are caught in a never-ending cycle of misery and displeasure with life until their dying day. Then, as we are about to leave for our homeward journey, we say, "What is the Point" what was my life all about. I could have achieved so much. I always wanted to play the piano, write a book, paint a landscape. Alas, too late was the cry.

Reading these words is a time for self-reflection. Go to the mirror right now and ask yourself

Am I happy?

Am I content?

Am I getting the best I can out of myself?

What would we do if we had a next-door neighbor who kept sticking his head over the garden fence and continually talked about all the negatives of life? Look at the bad weather. Look at the scandal of the politicians. Look at the fall in the stock market. On and on, day after day.

What a meddler — we would tell him to shut up in no uncertain terms.

Why do we continually allow our minds to treat us in this manner?

Why do we attach our thoughts to things that have no lasting importance?

Why lose the precious moments of Joy in a negative maze?

As long as we only see ourselves in the perspective of our memories, we will not be able to change. We have to release the old attachments of memories and desires.

We need new actions to feed our memory new thoughts.

We need to refresh the old brain box.

We need to spring clean the cobwebs of negativity.

We need to start a new way of thinking.

We need to purify the gray matter.

It is no longer adequate to say I want to lose weight because as long as we want to lose weight we never will. We have to forget about our physique and just start to eat healthy, nutritious food in a limited manner. This will enable us to lose weight with no effort — no fad diets.

We need to stop saying I wish I could give up smoking and drinking. We replace those thoughts and say if my lungs, liver and heart could vote would they elect me as their leader. We need to tune into our bodies' channels to feel what our organs are feeling and let them lead us.

Each tissue and sinew in our bodies sends messages to the brain, be silent and listen attentively. Sit in total silence and let the universal intelligence that is connected to every cell and atom in our body direct our path. Release the ego's hold. Acknowledge there is a higher intelligence that can guide our path, which can shine its light. Master the Mind of the Ego.

We begin to direct our attentiveness to our Soul and know we are loved and need no substitute from the outside world. We were always loved. We will always be loved, from now until eternity, for the eternal is here and now. We are the beloved ones and are embraced in Joy.

We no longer seek the attention of humankind for approval. We now live on a higher level of existence. We live in the realms of the eternal, beside an infinite stream of Divine Bliss.

In love with Love... In Joy with Joy.

What is the point?

Love and Joy is the point of no return -- No return to addictions and Illusions of a short-lived finite world directed by a meddling neighbor.

To determine our most precious assets we need to ask ourselves what we value the most.

SLICE TWENTY FIVE
Feast For The Senses

Our health is more precious than any diamond and yet we allow it to deteriorate out of ignorance of True information and attach our thoughts to misinformation. We know smoking and drinking alcohol is a quick way to a hospital bed but still many folks say this is what they enjoy. New scientific evidence is educating us to the fact eating: meat, dairy, candies, chocolate, cookies, cakes, sodas and foods containing hydrogenated fats & artificial flavors may lead to illnesses such as cancer and heart attacks.

The foods we are eating, eats away at our life span.

Most of us know fresh fruit, vegetables, whole grains, nuts, Etc., should be our wholesome diet. But we keep eating the toxic food until we make ourselves ill and die too soon.

They say we are what we eat. In truth we are what we think.

The question then becomes; who is directing us to eat all the wrong foods and why do we continue to do so even when we now know it is shortening our life. Our perception of living a happy life has been built with a good education but little wisdom.

If we are treating our bodies in this manner it is quite likely we are treating our minds in the same way. It is quite possible that negative thoughts have a knock on effect and make us look for a substitution for happiness.

We are wined and dined with a mass of information on the negative side of life. We bear a grudge, we seek revenge, we are resentful, we worry and become anxious, we hold fear and hatred. Frustrations and devastation's pile on the agony. We feed ourselves a banquet of negative toxic thoughts. This is all stored in our memories and seeps into our conscious minds on a daily basis. We have allowed people & events we have no control over in this world to control our minds.

On top of all this we also have the media to contend with.

We allow the advertising media to brainwash us into thinking we desire certain tastes and this will bring us Joy. We sample the goods and they taste real good. We now educate our subconscious to trigger a desire of harmful but tasty food whenever we have a negative thought.

This is done automatically and the desire takes on its own momentum so we get cravings for unhealthy food most of the time. Our bodies tell our minds to crave tasty types of food. It just becomes routine and "Normal" to eat all the unhealthy foods and when someone comes along to advise on a healthier way of eating they are called a crank and dismissed from our minds.

Then one day we become sick, we take many types of medication and it may relieve the symptoms for a while but negative thoughts persist.

We now become sick from the side effects of the medication on top of the toxic thoughts.

What a concoction of poison we have found for ourselves.

Our minds & bodies have a great defense system and some people can take more stress than others, so there will always be a few people that can abuse their bodies and seemingly get away with it. They really don't. They just have a higher pain threshold and strong Genes. But the majority of folks crack under the stresses and strains of unhealthy living.

I began by saying our health is more precious than any diamond and yet we allow it to deteriorate out of ignorance of information. So what is the information we need to keep the healthy mind & body most of us were born with.

Every cell in our bodies has been coded over millions of years of evolution and is programmed to think for itself. Our main powerhouse is our brain and the neuron receptors are connected to every cell in our bodies. Our eating habits reflect our thinking therefore we are what we think and take shape from what we eat. The Intelligence that coded our bodies in the first place, is available to guide us throughout our lives. Our pure potential of awareness is called our soul and is a part of Spirit that lodges in our bodies whilst we have a physical presence here on Earth. When we clear our minds we listen to our Soul. The Unified Force Field of Universal Intelligence (God) is our true identity and when we listen to our true selves Health Wealth & Happiness is our reward.

We find we need no reason to be happy all our time on earth.

Joy becomes a state of being.

Joy heals wounds and repairs bodies.

JOY means Just Obey Yourself

Your true self is a part of Universal-Intelligent-Energy we call God.

Humanity is a metaphysical strand in the web of life With this knowledge people the world over can live a natural life in-tune with nature.

The alien ego beings disappear and the human being once again live in peace and harmony with all things bright and beautiful.

Now we are fed on Soul Food.

A Feast for the Senses.

Truth lives at the base of all pools of thought. If the ponds are congested with illusions & delusions the truth will seldom surface.

SLICE TWENTY SIX
The Minds Delusions

Are we on the correct path in life? Who knows the truth? What are the answers to life's mysteries? Well folks here are the answers. We All possess the keys to unlock the puzzles of life. How do we access them? Well, here's how.

Firstly, let's stand in front of a full-length mirror. Now take off all your cloths. Do you like what you see?

Are you more than ten pounds over weight?

You are! Why? How did you get into this state?

Who are you listening to?

Who or what is it, inside your head, promoting actions to give your body its shape

Have you got a deluded mind-set hiding in there, feeding you with all the wrong information?

If you have been out of shape for quite a while, there is a good chance you have an illness festering inside all the toxicity of overload. If you do not have one at this moment, there is s good chance one is waiting in the overloaded cells. Does it sound a little ugly? What do we do when we get sick?

They say one ounce of prevention is worth a pound of cure. So do we want to continue to look at ourselves in the mirror and not take the appropriate action? What can we do? The good news is, it's never too late to change ourselves.

Let's go back to the mirror. Now take a close look at your face. Does it radiate Joy and Serenity?

Is your face a constant ray of sunshine for others to see? No!

Why not? ... Ask yourself-Why Not?

Keep on asking until some answers start to come to your mind. Your face reflects the state of wellness inside the body. If you're not satisfied with the answers your mind is giving you, keep on asking questions to yourself.

You will find the answers if you keep on asking. If you are a smoker ask your lungs and heart "if they could vote would they elect you as your leader" Wait for the answer. If your drink alcohol ask your liver and brain cells "Would you elect me as your leader" Wait for the answer. If you are over weight, ask your body cells "would you elect me as your leader" If the answer is "No, I would not elect you as my leader.".... Get a new leader!! Get in touch with the genius within you that can provide the answers and listen to the inner voice's guidance.

You see you had the answers all along. You just didn't know how to ask. Faithful answers send mystical signals to seed a life filled with love, harmony, serenity and most importantly of all J-O-Y.

Let's look at the shape of our body. Let's look at the shape of our mind and let's get our house in order. The good news is we all have the power to make changes for the better. Start at home and start now. Remember "Enjoy Yourself It's Later Than You Think" and we can only truly enjoy ourselves, once we get our house (Mind) in order. Let's turn the bad and the ugly into... The good and beautiful so that we can help all humanity to enjoy life. Just ask your soul, which means just ask your authentic self. Now let's get rid of the minds delusions and truly enjoy life.

People have become gullible lambs who are taken for a ride by avaricious lions.

SLICE TWENTY SEVEN
In You and Me

On a day so rare, so precious as this, it is in-deed a trespass, to disturb such bliss, temporal virtue, in such splendid scene, so hard to resist, but pure, as pure, as pure, can be, beyond this moment, we need to see, elegant natural truths, silently attach, to you and me, so gather round my trusty ladies 'n genteel men, I have a forgotten tale to tell, but yet again, history conveys, it was all so different then, A time ago, people once heard, babbling brooks sing, materialism unknown, there was no such thing, helping each other, was no disgrace, people enjoyed, living in grace, no change of face, in the credit of time, the bells of religion, still yet to chime, no need to boost, prestigious personality, no deceitful cloaks, of personal vanity, no intellectual priories, contracting infamy, no false illusions, attached to identity, 'twas a time of freedom, without ego's restraint, now regarded, as old fashioned 'n quaint, still, close your mortal eyes, beyond individual notoriety, discover melodic visions, each note floating, on celestial sea, laurels of clarity, illuminated, by inner divinity, waves of glorious innocence, flowing, in sublime beauty, treasures of eternal oneness, silent tides, in you and me.

A still mind, with crystal clear emptiness, travels in a first class carriage of gladness though all the daily confusion ... A busy mind journeys in steerage, going around so fast; it fabricates its own disorder.

SLICE TWENTY EIGHT
The Peaceful War of Existence.

The word 'WAR' seems to frighten many folks. I must admit that those that wage war need to understand that there are no winners - just some lose less. Does that mean we do not have the right to defend ourselves from aggressors? Can we appease or gratify an enemy intent on our death? Certainly not, the opposite is true. We need to understand what a credible battle means and why it is necessary. We have to comprehend whom we are and how our bodies function to gain answers. Every day 'war comes into our lives even though we are unaware of its presence and presents as a 'war.'

The human being is born with a flight, fight mentality. It served us well many moons ago but today it plays havoc with our immune systems. In to-day's world, we are taught to live by social graces and to operate in a civilized manner. This means loving thy neighbor. All is well until we live next door to the neighbors from hell. What then, do we run or fight? Let's take a closer look at our bodies for truthful answers.

Every moment we are alive there is a war going on inside ourselves. Good germs are fighting bad germs. Good Bacteria is fighting bad bacteria. Good cells are fighting free radical formed bad cells...A constant battleground. Armies are lined up and millions of bad guys are eliminated. Should the bad guys ever win, we will capture a sickness and die. Before our passing we might have to wage war on a cancer or some other debilitating dis-ease. It could turn out to be a long drawn out battle. Do we just say I want peace and surrender or do we fight? Do we value life?

In our lives, our bodies will fight many battles just to stay alive. Fights are part of nature. If a butterfly is helped out of its cocoon, it will die. It has to fight to free itself - then it can take wings and fly. Nature is formed by the survival of the fittest. Severe weather, earthquake, etc. kill life and then new life grows. The old is replaced by the new. Our bodies are part of nature and function in the physical world we live, fueled by spirit. When it boils down to evil guys trying to kill the good guys what do we do? Can we afford to be impassive, unresponsive or indifferent?

The obvious question to ask is, "Who are the good Guys"? Well let's go back to our bodies. Who are the good guys there? The cells that want to destroy us or the one's who want to keep us healthy and flourishing? We need to grasp spirits meaning for solutions. Spirit has designed the show called nature and we are part of nature.

Our egos will give us the tendencies to destroy out of a need to possess and hold power. This comes in all shapes and sizes - in so many ways. Politics, religion, science, man made laws, etc. all can hold extreme dogma. When it turns into a mad Dog-ma, it needs to be put down and war becomes the only way, once the dogma has festered into such dis-ease that it will destroy everybody. Many free-radical, bad cells of terror will develop, and their propaganda and lies will darkly envelope all the morality and goodness of humankind.

Cells of bad terrorists called fundamentalists wish to kill innocent healthy cells called justice and freedom. In the middle of this battle lives unaware, gullible cells of people that want peace with no action, no war. They will sacrifice themselves out of futile ignorance of Spirits power to protect. In the same unaware way, folks kill themselves out of the foods they eat and the worry and anxiety they inhale.

A war must be fought to combat evil's dis-ease. The good guys must eventually win or there will be no one left on earth to know the difference between good and bad. Once we bury spirit, we bury humankind. Life on earth for humans will cease to exist.

We cannot allow rabid dogmas and misguided radical teachings to take us down a path of no return. If we do, then a nuclear holocaust will develop. The remains of the day will be a pile of ashes to ashes and dust to dust. Before we reach that stage, we must put our guardianship in God and invest in Spirits irrevocable trust. What great company to invest our time in. The harvest will yield; One Planet, One People, One God.

When we accept these words as our truth, folks will no longer feel the need to prove their point. Belligerent humans will be replaced with the peaceful war of existence. That war is against poverty, disease, pollution and any other acts that take life prematurely. Spirit will provide the means to save lives, if we listen without conditions, to the one true God. The motto from the founding fathers of America is "From the many one." We now need to turn that around and say "From the Holy One are born many, all content and gratified within Spirits intelligence of Love & Joy."

The more a person thinks they know, the less their choice become.

SLICE TWENTY NINE
Living By Laws of Nature.

Can our religious and scientific teachings help humanity to live a more authentic life in our modern breakneck-paced world? Well, let's become archaeologists and dig some genuine meaning out of the Bible." In the beginning there was light." Without light no-thing can grow. The Sun provides earth with light...And God said; "it was all good. "When we read the first few chapters in the Bible, we possess the opportunity to decode the story of Adam and Eve. This will supply us with a formula that adheres to the laws of nature/ spirit/universe..... so that all humanity can prosper in peaceful harmony.

When Eve handed Adam the apple from the Tree of Knowledge, Adam ate the forbidden fruit. They were both evicted from paradise by an angry landlord.

They broke a house rule. Now we can believe the story as is, or we can search a little deeper and find out what the author really meant by the story of Adam and Eve's disobedience. Eating forbidden fruit is a symbolic phrase meaning, we are doing something that goes against the Laws of Nature. Since the tabooed fruit came from the Tree Of Knowledge, it must mean that something unsavory happened to the whole of humanity many years ago.

Something effected humanities eviction from paradise. Now; what is it that lives in all our minds and takes away our happiness, peace of mind and contentment? What takes away our personal paradise? We do not have to search too far to find the answer.

Negative emotions that produce stressful reactions in our bodies are the forbidden fruits we digest every day of our lives. Most people die of dis-ease related illness. Despite being kept alive for many years on medications that have bad side effects, people still die of a dis-ease. Therefore; the only real cure from disease is to stop all the negative emotions.

We have to locate our endowed keys that unlock the gates into paradise. We need to reinstate our minds into a sanctuary of happiness, peace of mind and contentment. For that is the domicile nature designated humanity to inhabit. I doubt if there is not one sane person on planet earth that does not want to live in paradise. Most will say it is impossible; nevertheless, their first wish would be to live a happy, healthy life.

Let's get back to the Genesis of earth. In the beginning there was light (Sun, heat) Then there was volcanic actions as earth began to cool (fire.) Through the evolutionary process within the erosion of rocks (weather, fungi, bacteria, etc.,) soil was formed, permeated with a mass of organic life. In just one teaspoon of fertile soil exists forty-thousand different species of organic life. Within each specie lives one-hundred-million living organisms. A whole universe in one small spoon of dirt. With the heat from the sun and the water of the oceans, life seeded in the soil begins to grow. The rain (water.) cultivated the soil and it began to grow ferns and vegetation.

The growth became jungle congested with weeds and many plants that held back many more beautiful, exotic plants from growing. The seeds of exotic plants had been planted by evolution, but they found it difficult to grow because the stronger weeds held their space. Strong storms (water) and heat waves (fire) reduced the weeds to ashes and this gave the beautiful exotic plants the opportunity to blossom and flourish. In nature, destruction shapes construction.

From the spark within the seed came the bud...From the spark within the bud grew the flower. From the life within the flower...The seed.

And so the cycle continues, all without the aid of humans. Flowers live in paradise, so why aren't humans as intelligent as flowers? Humans are also grown from Spirits seed. So what ignorance is holding back humanities growth?

Just as the butterfly learnt how to escape from its cocoon, so humanity must learn how to escape from eating forbidden fruit (negativity). If anyone would help the butterfly from escaping from its cocoon, the butterfly would perish before it can escape and fly. It must withstand its ground (not violently struggle against nature) and wait for the cocoon to eventually weaken to set itself free. As it prods its way through the cocoon, it builds up the muscle and strength to exist as a beautiful butterfly. It enjoys the stages of metamorphism as it transforms into a beautiful butterfly.

No matter what hand life deals us, we must enjoy every experience. The negative emotions we digest are the weeds in our life that we need to grow through. They were not part of our original make up, for in the beginning "All Was Good" It only became bad when we stared to become more sophisticated and use our intellect in many ways nature did not intend. This gave rise to the "bad" things in life. The "bad things" are our hatreds, jealousies, anger, dogmas, selfishness ect.

If we could do an internal inspection on our intellectual brain, it would communicate that the emotions are real and the intellect is the master decision maker. However, if we could do a search on past generations, two million years ago, with similar brains, we would probably find there was a time when the brain only contained intelligence.

The intellect/ego was just a good idea waiting to form itself. We have come a long way since then, but is it progress to sacrifice our happiness and simplicity? Humanity has to accept the true facts of life. The intellect-ego is a learning tool of the mind to enhance our understanding of universal intelligence. It decodes intelligence that has always existed, even before the cosmos began. The intellect should not be a dominant force that shepherds human life into emotional distress.

In the real estate world there are three golden rules.....Location, location, location. And so it is with our minds. Where do we wish our thoughts to be located? In the Intellect/ego that is keen on eating many forbidden fruits (inauthentic information.) Or, do we wish to locate our thoughts in paradise, where nature's intelligence blends magnificently with human intelligence/intellect/ego. All for one and one for all.

Location-Location-Location...

Location one...Humanity can blossom as a radiant heavenly Orchid

Location two...Humanity can emit the aura of fragrant celestial Jasmine

Location three Humanity can feel as velvety as a divine rose petal.

Is it time you launch your beautiful intelligent wings of your mind and transform into a creative, ingenious human butterfly?

The location of your thoughts depends on whose garden you wish to plant the seeds of prosperity.

The solo intellects/egos world of "bad" or Natures/Spirits world of "Good" that guides the ego/intellect into paradise. Time to get out the excavator and do a little digging in the fields of authentic thought... Located in the exotic paradise gardens of your mind. Reap your harvest of Joy from the Love seeds you plant.

Treasure people as you would like to be savored. Allow the blossom of your smile to enliven all your fellow human prime mates. Learn the meaning of the word JOY and start to... enjoy yourself; it's later than you think!

In sleep, a connect mind charts enchanting courses for the coming day. A disconnected mind will lose its way.

SLICE THIRTY
Living Without Doubt.

Many times in our lives, we will come across folks who ridicule and insult others to hide their inadequacies. This lack of self-esteem comes from doubt of truthful living. They just do not know who or what to believe so they hit out at everyone who will not agree with their doubtfulness.

Anyone who lives with doubt can never be classed as a free thinker and thus become imprisoned within their own fantasy. They simply become procrastinators who never achieve anything worthwhile to pass on to their fellow human.

A free thinker comes to definite decisions and lives their truth to bring them and others Joy.

Freedom from Doubt... brings free thinkers. Edison never doubted he could make a light bulb. It took him 10,000 efforts to make it, but he had no doubts he would succeed.

Michael Angelo had no doubt about the beauty of the statue hidden in the marble. He chiseled away until was formed.

Did the first sailors ever doubt the world was round?

The creators truths are the only reality and no religion or science can change Gods creations. Doubt is only for the illusions of the ego and has no value to man or beast.

All the famous men and women had no doubt their truths would create lasting treasures. For they all knew it was not their own veracity but multi-dimensional universal truths.

There are only "The Truths of the Creator/Evolver," and we all encompass them. They make us co-creators/evolvers when we tune in and decode their magnificent messages of invention. They have always been in existence since the universe was formed and they are part of our very fiber.

Science and Religion may have differing view points, but they both go back to a source of creation/evolving that is infinite and eternal. They both base their truths on the same principals at source, but just express it in differing intellectual ways.

Where there is doubt... there can be no truth.

Without truth.... there is NO Freedom of Thought.

In tough times, spirited people with courage, ethics and kindness will find the best opportunities to help others.

SLICE THIRTY ONE
Spiritual Genes

Many people will declare humans are stuck with the genes they are born with. To some degree that is true for the first ten years of a child's life. That is because children are dependent on other people such as parents and teachers to look after their welfare. After the age of ten a child begins to mature mentally very quickly these days and can start to reaffirm or contradict the things it has been taught by religion, schooling, parents and friends. There is not much the child can do to change the environment it is in, but it can slowly change its view of life. Many children become rebellious and hit out at society because they know of no other way of getting their confusions and frustrations out of their system. Their emotions are sparked off by the double standards they constantly come across and find the only way to be heard is to do something that will shock society.

The vast majority of children find it is too much of a struggle to fight their conditioning and indoctrination and any thoughts of dissent is soon knocked out of them. They become typical normal people with all the normal dis-ease, aggravation, depression and anxiety. They will remark. What can I do it is in my genes, and so it is but it does not have to be that way and even physical genes can change over a period of time...But, the question is how do we change them?

Quite simply, the way to change the physical make-up of the mind & body is to find new creations to generate a cause and turn it into an effect. And what better way to produce a cause and effect than changing the way life is perceived and assumed to be. In other words, change the conscious minds conviction and persuasions so that it digests a new way of thinking that is as ageless as eternity...

Wow! Wouldn't that be great, but how do we do that?

Most people will say it is impossible to change the DNA, therefore fate and destiny cannot be altered ... For all those folks that think that way, it is true, because that is their truths ... But for any person who wants to contemplate a more joy filled life, with no worry or anxiety, there is a source of power that can regenerate new genes, that replace defective genes.

Before the physical mind and body can change, it first needs to be infused with spiritual genes. A new metaphysical angioplasty needs to be implanted from the subconscious mind and then drip- fed into the conscious mind over a period of time. As the new spiritual genes are manifested, it will materialize into a new paradigm of thought that can re-energize stale thought patterns, which have been the fountainhead of past irritation and dissent. In silent minds, new authentic of spirit seeds can be planted and sown. They will bloom and flourish with grace and compassion for all of humanity to savor. What better legacy can we leave to our children's children than spiritual genes, permeating with the wisdom of the universe?

Kind folks who try to create peace and forgiveness as their purpose do in-deed inherit the earth.

SLICE THIRTY TWO
Aspects of Philosophy

What does it mean to be a philosopher and what are the aspect of philosophy? Can professors and teachers apply universal wisdom with all subjects they teach? Do they know what universal intelligence is? If they do not have the connection to the source of all intelligence, how can they apply true meaning and good intent to every subject taught in schools and universities?

Whilst the questions seem simple enough to answer (and they are), in the academic world of philosophy, it has become almost impossible to accept the answers within a three hundred and sixty degree universal point of view. That is probably due to the fact philosophy that is published in academic journals has to follow certain guidelines and procedures that contains scholastic logic and reasoning....But the logic and reasoning of to-days intellectual brain has very little connection to original ancient philosophy or the manner in which humans evolved. Most academic philosophies can be compared to a large prize marrow that has won best in show. It may be very attractive to people interested in pretty marrows, but it is only for looking at and not grown for human digestion. So what does philosophy mean? Lets look how Webster's dictionary defines the word philosophy.....

Phi·los·o·phy

I : all learning exclusive of technical precepts and practical arts (2) : the sciences and liberal arts exclusive of medicine, law, and theology <a doctor of philosophy> (3) : the 4-year college course of a major seminary b (I) : archaic : Physical Science (2) : Ethics c : a discipline comprising as its core logic, aesthetics, ethics, metaphysics, and epistemology
2 a : pursuit of wisdom b : a search for a general understanding of values and reality by chiefly speculative rather than observational means c : an analysis of the grounds of and concepts expressing fundamental beliefs

3 a : a system of philosophical concepts b : a theory underlying or regarding a sphere of activity or thought <the philosophy of war> <philosophy of science> 4 a : the most general beliefs, concepts, and attitudes of an individual or group b : calmness of temper and judgment befitting a philosopher © 2001 by Merriam-Webster, Incorporated.

So we can claim philosophy should contain the total knowledge known to humankind, in the pursuit of wisdom, within a balanced order.

Core logic and reason, aesthetics, righteousness, metaphysics, concepts, epistemology and wisdom should be the ingredients of.........

Analytic Philosophy
A trend in philosophical analysis that seeks to resolve philosophical perplexity by revealing sources of puzzlement in the misunderstanding of ordinary language
Moral Philosophy
Ethics and the study of human conduct and values
Natural Philosophy
Natural Science; Especially: Physical Science
Ordinary Language Philosophy A trend in philosophical analysis that seeks to resolve philosophical perplexity by revealing sources of puzzlement in the misunderstanding of ordinary language
Philosophy of Life
An overall vision of or attitude toward life and the purpose of life.

All of the above categories contain the word philosophy, therefore all should hold core logic, reason, aesthetics, righteousness, metaphysics, epistemology and most of all wisdom, but in many cases they do not.

Over the past two hundred years many new philosophies have taken on a world of their own and the philosophers who endorse them are as dogmatic as any fundamental religious follower.

With such a vast assortment of different types of philosophy why has segments of academia taken upon itself to be judge and jury and pick only what they term as philosophy and more or less ignore everything that does not conform to their narrow tunnel vision of philosophy? What happened to simple authentic wisdom?

Could it be the ego/intellect of the academic mind wants to capture philosophy, hold it hostage and thereby only publish works that are read by an inner circle of academics who want to believe they are a special breed that has a higher view of life? If this is the case, nothing could be further from authentic fact....Ivory towers have never been a safe place to hide away and pretend the rest of the world does not exist. Education should be embraced by the universal source of intelligence that gave the professors a brain in the first place. The application of universal laws should be structured into every subject, taught to every student, in every place of learning.

For example; If professors are teaching mathematics they should teach the student how to apply math's so that they can help humanity to progress.... Not so that they can become financial directors and use their mathematical skills to cheat millions of people out of their hard, honestly earned money.

The greed of large corporation and the sensationalism in the media is proof universal intelligence was not part of their education.

Let's contemplate the aspects of philosophy in simple terms...

If we wanted to research nutritional and healthy eating characteristics we could read many books, journals and magazines to find out what is good and what is bad for our diet...on the other hand, if we use simple authentic wisdom that projects the philosophy of healthy eating, maybe we can sum that up in one short sentence...

Eat natural foods in a balanced manner and don't overeat.

Who could argue with that? And if the meaning in the sentence is accepted and lived, it would allow the follower to eat healthily. No fad diets required. What could be simpler?

So with that in mind, what if we want to research philosophical understanding, we can read a mountain of books, journals and magazines on different philosophies or we can sum philosophy up in one short sentence.

Consume natural universal thoughts in a balanced, Joy filled, wise, loving, authentic manner and don't over-think your actuality.

This sentence contains core logic and reason, aesthetics, righteousness, metaphysics, concepts and epistemology..... So why can't everyone follow it? Well, it may take a little more debate to locate the source of natural universal thought.

When a human being lives on the same level of intelligence as a fish, bird, insect, animal and plant they live naturally...

- A fish: can locate a destination three thousand mile away from its departure point without a map or compass...How many philosophers can do that?
- A bird: can fly in perfect synchronicity will all its mates and each one takes the lead and knows where their destination is located. No compass required. How many philosophers can do that?
- Insects: such as Ants can carry ten times their own weight, work in harmony for the betterment of their colony and it is one for all and all for one....How many philosophers can do that?
- Animals: posses many in-build skills and without the aid of an education, can perform great mastery in hostile surrounds. They retain a keen sense of surrounding danger and can move at swift speeds with no aid of machinery. They enjoy their life on earth with just nature supplying all their requirements...How many philosophers can do that?
- Plants: provide food and oxygen to all life forms on earth and embrace universal intelligence with no questions asked....How many philosophers can do that?

Humanity can live as natural as all other life forms if they adopt an authentic philosophy that embraces its source of evolving/creation. Within a thought realm that feeds the intellectual part of the brains intelligence, the human being can use its superior intellectual logic and reasoning to work out a blueprint to live in harmony and peace with no division and no different philosophies, religions or sects. If we all live for one and one for all, sharing, giving and caring, wars will cease and humanity will advance as nature intended...In synchronicity with all other life forms on earth.

Who can argue with that wisdom? What could be more authentically simple? What could be more universally profound?

What other aspects of academic philosophy could be more important to the survival of humanity?

Everybody is born into paradise with a simple mind ... All too soon; most are evicted by ignorance masquerading as cleverness.

SLICE THIRTY THREE
Alone in a Sacred Place

In the spirit compass of creation resides the 361 degree of truth, latitudes of now... longitudes of here, I know not where I am; yet, feel warm n secure in soul comfort, alone in a sacred place, a deep sense of nothingness probes deeper n deeper, free of body and mind I float in unceasing circles of divine bliss, waves of unfathomable joy-filled solitude wash over the essence of my being, mesmerizing images cultivate white love lights of devotion, inner n outer fields of inspiration encourage tones n filters of magical beauty, this is a mystical wonderland, open all hours, within infinite array's of splendor.

In life there is only one demon to master and it does not live outside our thoughts.

SLICE THIRTY FOUR
Welcome to Fantasy Land.

When was the last time you visited a theme park? Did you enjoy it?

Most people love to go to a theme park and escape the hum-drum chores of everyday living. How real are theme parks? All those fascinating furry costumed creatures that come up to us and give us a big hug... How cute they look, but how real are they?

Within an eye to a young child, they are very real, but through the view of adulthood, they are just a person in a costume...Right? Well, not exactly, for many times, we use our imagination for just that one-day and we go along with the fantasy. After all, that is the fun of going into a theme park...To indulge in the fantasy ... is it not?

We allow our imagination to go back to our childhood and we enjoy all the fun of the fair. At the end of the day, we are tired but very contented with all the release of worry and tensions the fantasy has relieved. But...we do not live in fantasy worlds do we? We have to go back out into the "real world," to face all the negativity and dangers of modern day living, or do we?

So, what is real and what is fantasy in our everyday lives? Worry and anxiety seem real enough when there are events in our lives that take on harmful emotional stress. Being in debt, sickness, death of a loved one, all this stuff will play havoc with our enjoyment of life and turn happiness into sorrow. Debt, illness and lack of joy can be avoided if we know the true, authentic paths to follow, but death of our physical form is a certainty...You can bet your life on it! But ... what is life? And how real is death?

Well, the physical presence on earth disappears. The ego/intellect that was so worried about its appearance, other peoples gossip, making lots of money, keeping up with the Jones's, world events, family arguments and a host over other "Important stuff" will all disappear like smoke...Just as if it was all a fantasy? A theme on life...in a park of drama perhaps?

It sure is a shame most folks forgot their lines they were given at birth and tried to ad-lib a script fabricated by self-torment and mental-torture. The fantasy they enacted really seemed like reality, but since all finite substances are glued together atoms, fed by chemicals such as serotonin and dopamine, they are bound to come unstuck eventually and the "reality" fades into oblivion...The good news is the tangible authentic be-ing will never fade away. The true essence of a human-being is a constant flow of intelligent energy that cannot disappear. We label it a soul, but such identities cannot describe the indescribable...That has to be experienced.

So, is it time to get real now? .... To rediscover the authentic life that is projected here on earth and throughout eternity. Is it time to take off our fluffy costumes, our masks, our facade and to live as our authentic self. Is there any difference between eternity and the now existence? If you say; Yes there is, then you are living in a fantasy theme park, but this one has a long dark shadow that turns happiness into grief. It exists only in a will-o'-the-wisp called ego.

OK...enough already! ... I guess it is time to cut out the Non-Sense of the ego/intellect and to turn on...tune in...To our S- SENSE! The Spirit of a True Soul. Now that's a valid existence that experiences how to live in infinite Love & Joy! A design, within a subject, within a point, within a theme, within a dream, within a fantasy land...Enjoy it all from within! But understand... What is not born....cannot die. The eternal soul will nourish our life on earth ... for without the soul ... there is no life....Just a Fantasy of Delusions.

Before anyone can genuinely change their mind they need to get to grips with the chooser of their choices.

SLICE THIRTY FIVE
A Life & Death Situation.

Most folks have a virus protector on our computer. Unfortunately, the world is full of sick-minded people, so we need to be very cautions and guard against many attacks. But what shield do we possess to help our minds cope with the stresses and strains of modern day living?

We are living as a human being, but we are in essence a loving soul. The essence is eternal whereas the human beings mind & body is a temporary identity. A few weeks ago, I was asked to explain the sensations of the soul by a delightful lady.

I started by saying;

A soul is the essence of intelligent energy that recognizes true wisdom within the senses of Love and Joy. The soul becomes part of the physical human being the moment the first cell is born. It is the true "life" identity of a human. Just look at a babies face when it has food and comfort. It embodies a pure bundle of joy.

The lady then asked me, "What about death? Doesn't that take away our joy? Is anything left?"

I responded;

There can never be death of a soul. The body expires but intelligent energy cannot disappear. Joy is the core understanding of a soul. The only true feelings are love and joy and all the positive feelings that grow from them.

Once we are aware of our love & joy in our physical life, then the spirit of past loved ones are sparked in our minds. We are aware there presence is "Alive" and connected to our souls. We are still connected to all the loved ones who have transcended back into spirit.

This understanding should be the true mental picture of the myth called "life & death," otherwise we will just hold a memory of a physical being and that brings a loss and sadness. We will feel a loss, which attaches to a negative emotion, instead of our souls joy. We love our family and friends, but love is not a possession. There are no permanent structures in a physical life. Why concentrate our thoughts on a finite individual that is a temporary visitor. Isn't it better to be aware of our continuous true self?

She then asked me; Do you really want to say "The ONLY true feelings are Love and Joy?" Doesn't this invalidate people that are feeling other things such as grief, sadness, loss and anger right now? Those feelings are indeed also very real, necessary for the grieving process and "true"...aren't they?

I Responded;

Only in the eyes of the physical beings conditioning dwells grief and suffering. This ego (Ease God Out) image of ourselves is only a temporary condition and not reality. We cannot live by such basic emotions, or we will waste most of our life in a negative thought mist. This may sound harsh, but the opposite is true. To live in joy, spreads joy, to live with grief, spreads grief. Giving joy is caring. Spreading grief is selfish. We grieve for our loss, not for the loved one, for their physical presence has gone.

There is a big difference in emotions and feelings. We can only hold grief when there is a loss. Physically there is a loss and our emotions feel that loss. In our true state there can never be a loss for spirit cannot die, for it was not born. It flows through us as the wind brushes our cheek. That is our true identity. The whole of the cosmos is our domain. How can we grieve over an eternal energy force that we are? It makes no sense to cry and go against the realities of infinite wisdom.

The emotions that seem so real are part of our ego's view of the world and not real at all. Reality means lasting and nothing in the physical lasts. This is such a deep subject that many folks take a lifetime to learn and then it is too late. Most people never do comprehend the true meaning of "life & death."

Folks should continually ask probing questions and the more questions we ask, the clearer our reality becomes. The ONLY true feelings are love & joy. There can be no other reason to exist on earth without these feelings. We are not put on earth to suffer as many religions preach.

Over many thousands of years, we have been trained to believe grieving is a normal response to the death of a loved one...Especially a sudden death. But that does not mean it is natural to grieve. To understand it is like peeling an onion. Each layer will make us cry until we get to the end. Once we eat it, we will stop crying and just enjoy it's flavor and goodness. After a while we learn, if we cook it first, then peel each layer, we will not cry. Why live life in the raw?

We need to accept whom we truly are and the recipe for that takes time and practice. If we live with half-baked ideas, we will get indigestion very often. If we live only by emotions, we will cry very often. We will all feel negative emotions, for that is how our bodies have evolved.

The fight or flight emotions we originally felt, are today replaced with many other emotions that injure our immune systems and put us in an early grave. Our minds have not adjusted to modern day living and some religious rules & regulations only make matters worse. The spiritual essence of each religion is pure, but mankind changes it to suit its own power base.

The simple answer to the meaning of life is, `God put us on earth to enjoy every second, no matter what chaos, catastrophes and tragedies surround us. Now who wants to argue with God?

If we do, we will cry and grieve a lot. When we walk with Spirit in each step we take, no harm can befall us, so what is there to be unhappy about? Health, Wealth and Joy will flow freely if we allow nature to take its course. Once we can accept our true identity, we can live as member of the universe. What is the point of subsisting detached from a higher reality, as an ego be-ing, with no club card into spirits truths? A soul's energy... is life's potency. Where there's life, there lives a soul. Our sole purpose is to enjoy. What are you waiting for? After all; it is not as though it is a life or death situation?

May you go from strength to strength in Divine Bliss.

SLICE THIRTY SIX
Walking on a Path of Life.

We set out walking along a route where one foot walks on a sidewalk that is slowly ascending, taking us to higher levels of wisdom. Whilst the other foot walks on the road that maintains a flat, drab and weary surface, taking us ever deeper into negative emotions.

Eventually we will get to a point where we have to make a choice. Do we raise both feet up onto the elevated sidewalk and continue to ascend to higher levels of wisdom's joy? Or, do we keep both feet on the road, on the lower level of worry and anxiety (knowing we are walking where angels fear to tread)?

If we stay on the emotional road, we will keep sinking in the negative gutter and when it rains heavily,(tragic events) we may get washed away (dark days beyond our control). We also risk being hit by careless drivers. (Other aggressive, bullying humans, out for an argument)If we decide to keep both feet on the sidewalk of love & joy, we can promenade in safety and watch all the wonderful scenery (God's Gifts) whilst we go about our daily business.

We cannot go though life in doubt with one foot in one camp (skepticism and mistrust) and another foot in a different camp (faith and devotion). Life makes us make choices. The high path is one with Spirits safety and wonderment. The low road is governed by a stand alone ego, thwart with many negative, stressful, sickness inducing dangers, so why take risks?

Stroll in peace and harmony on the serene, tranquil, high side of life, via the "curb of negativity" and let's keep our mind out of the "negative gutter press of sensationalism." We may not be able to change the world right now, but we can change our minds, by living with the wisdom of a higher reality. Life passes us by with each tick of the clock...Is it time to walk on the high side?

For...Just a Moment or Two.

When we have to live life waiting for the approval of others, we will wait an eternity.

To live life with Gods intent is to observe life through a clear, open mind.

It is;

Always open to... a new relationship, for a moment or two.

Always open to... a fresh recipe, for a moment or two,

Always open to ... an original idea, for a moment or two,

Always open to ... an unfamiliar landscape, for a moment or two,

Always open to ... discover inventive creations, for a moment or two,

Always open to ... embrace nature, for a moment or two,

Always open to.... observe a sunset, for a moment or two,

Always open to.....a maestros music, for a moment or two,

Always open to... picturing life through a babies eyes, for a moment or two,

Always open to... visualize life through a teenagers eyes, for a moment or two,

Always open to... experience life through a parents eyes, for a moment or two,

Always open to... feel life through a grandparents eyes, for a moment or two,

For life passes so quickly, truly, mortals only have a taste for a moment or two, dancing upon the clock face of creation.

Then "Blink"... It's gone!!

The High————Way....Is the True-Eternal-Way.

Knowing what you know now, if you could change three events/things from the past what would they be?

SLICE THIRTY SEVEN
Monkeying Around With the Truth.

For the past few million years' human beings evolved into the species that exists today. What we observe is six billion people on a planet who all believe they live a normal life in their environment. And indeed they do...they all live a normal life, but how natural is that? How many humans live a natural life as nature intended? Has the evolutionary system allowed humans to fall into a pit of ignorance that could result in the disappearance of humanity? Perhaps if we can gleam some information from other species, we may see a little clearer our own folly and make amends.

I was watching a PBS program on evolution . One section of the program was a study on our closest relatives on earth, the apes and our similarities in two groups of apes in particular. Chimpanzees and Bonobos are the nearest existing relatives to humans. Many attributes of the apes within their societies, culture, mentality and intricate social interdependence are comparable to human society in general. Both groups of apes are intricately connected, even though they live in different intellectual structures.

The Chimpanzees are dominated by the most aggressive male and many fights continually erupt. The aggressive male physically injures many of the group so that he can keep his supremacy. (I wonder if Saddam parents were monkeying around?)

In the Bonobo society it seems they are only interested in eating food and making love all day long. (Mama Mia!! The Italian connection?) Two groups of apes look very similar in appearance but have evolved in different ways.

And so it is with human society. Humankind has evolved according to the environment and location of their community. For many thousands of years in the Middle East, the human power menu has delivered many wars and aggressions. Holy wars in God's name springs up on a regular basis whenever one group wish to dominate another group. Over time people moved from these regions to populate Europe, then the America's.

Today in the Middle East nothing has changed except the aggression has become more diabolical. Very few counties have democracy, public executions are enacted and suicide bombers disappear in a blast of insane glory along with many innocent people. This is now normal, but how natural is it?

Today in America, we live in societies where people are shot and killed for no reason. This is now normal, but how natural is it?

1. Today in America, folks are robbed and assaulted in broad daylight by barbarians. This is now normal, but how natural is it?

2. Today in America, women of all ages are mercilessly raped by uncouth animals. This is now normal, but how natural is it?

3. Today in America, irrational children kill their teachers and classmates. This is now normal, but how natural is it?

4. Today in America, vulgar clergymen sexually abuse young boys. This is now normal, but how natural is it?

5. Today in America, mindless humans inflict air pollution on mass populations, which becomes responsible for the deaths of millions over time. This is now normal, but how natural is it?6.

6 Today in America, heart dis-ease and cancer kill millions of people through stress and bad diet. This is now normal, but how natural is it?

7 Today in America, a few savage executives can rob millions of unaware people out of their hard earned life savings. This is now normal, but how natural is it?

I could make a list that will reach from the East coast, to the West coast of events, actions and sickness that are now considered normal, but how natural is it?

How do humans differ from their close relatives the Chimps? Maybe only by the fact Chimps do not have human resources to cause greater mayhem in their society. My! Oh! My! What a wretched variety of normal, uneasy, complicated beings we have evolved into… What unnatural traits of mayhem we have adapted over thousands of years.

Is it now locked in our DNA, in our Genes?

Can nothing be done to eliminate our normal way of life so that we can become natural again, as nature intended?

Is there any hope" Maybe a glimmer of Light?

- Normality cannot be conquered by normal.
- Another fire cannot douse a fire.
- A flood cannot be drained by water.
- Ignorance of identity cannot be enlightened by the ignorant brains

Many people will get sick at some stage of their life and eventually die of dis-ease. At best, medication or surgery will give a band-aid remedy that will fix up the immediate problem, but cannot eliminate the cause of dis-ease. No, it takes something else to see through the charade, the masquerades, the pretense, the mask of normality covering all the evil and depravity of a normal human society. It Takes the Eye Of Natural Human Spirit to cleanse normal people.

Perhaps we can raise our standards to those of the Bonobo apes, so that we learn to share our food and wisdom with the whole world, so nobody feels the needs to rob and kill. We can learn to spread our love to every nation on earth, so nobody feels unloved or unwelcome on mother earth. The French word for good is "Bon" Surely, we can learn to live equal to the Bonobos and listen to our Good Boss ... The Creator. Let's all progress from normal ignorance and advance to natural truth. For only the Creator know what is natural and what is true ... 'Bon Appetite'

The best way to get rid of inner pests is to spray them with truthful philosophy... It never flunks the test of time and passes every exam of life with honors.

SLICE THIRTY EIGHT
Mother Angel

One of the strongest devotions of physical unconditional love is the one between a mother and her son. I was fortunate to have a mother who doted on her son, no matter how boisterous or cheeky he was and I doted on her. She also happened to be one of life's true Angels and would run around helping anyone in the neighborhood who needed a helping hand. Wherever there was distress, my mother was present to bring her affection and caring. She also worked full time at home as an out-worker sewing buttons on raincoats and being paid a pittance.

Unfortunately, I only had twenty-three years to experience, savor and embrace my mother's physical love, for she died far too young at the tender age of fifty-five. She suffered many illness before she died, all brought about by the stress and strains of worrying about other peoples misfortunes and adversities. She never had time to take care of herself and was always disquieted about the well being of all the people she knew and loved. I never ever heard her say a bad word about anyone she met. Florence Levy was a real Florence Nightingale reincarnate. Even today forty-two years after her passing, the few people left who knew her, still speak in glowing terms of the deeds of an unsung hero....my mum. She was a True Angel.

The last five years of her life was spent in and out of different hospitals. Whilst her health was declining, I fell in love with a seventeen year old girl and got married. I was just nineteen year old and fathered two children in the first eighteen months. I was not sure where they came from, but it was sure was a great deal of fun finding out. I also started my own little textile business a few weeks before I got married. I had just sixty dollars in my pocket (my worldly wealth) to buy a few cloth remnants, which I sold at the local town market. I was not taking any risks at that time, for when you have next to nothing (monetary speaking)...the only place to go is up.

My divine Joy was my treasure and it was (And still is) the force that would take me through all the trials and tribulations of the approaching years of disheartenment, although at the time I could not analyze it ... I could just simply live it.

So, here I was newly married with two children and all my spare time was spent visiting my mum in hospital and in a sick bed at home. The last two years were the most traumatic as she underwent four major operations. The last one was on her liver and she never recovered from the operating theater. The day she died was an utter devastation and tears streamed down my face from morning till night and into the wee hours. I remember sleeping for a couple of hours and then waking up to the nightmare of my dear mother's funeral. In the Jewish religion you are buried the day after you die. There is also the custom of sitting 'Shiva' for a week for prayers and mourning.

My mourning was so deep, that no customs could help ease the pain. Heart rendering waves of grief surged all through my very being the whole of the funeral day. For a young frivolous, simple man who always lived in joy, the suffering was an utter disintegration of all my senses. The spirit wrenching grieving was beyond anything I could have imagined. At the grave side I had to shovel dirt onto my mother's coffin which was lowered six feet into the ground. The thud of the dirt hitting the cheap wooden casket lives with me still thirty-five years later.

That night was the first night of sitting 'Shiva' and all the members of the family and friends came to the house at seven thirty for prayers and a few words of condolence from the rabbi. I was in no mood for formalities. I hardly spoke or was even aware anyone was in the room. That night in bed my head hit the pillow and I went into a deep, deep sleep. I know I embodied some strange dreams that night, but in all honesty I cannot remember what they were.

The next day all the tears had dried up inside and as the day progressed I was feeling lighter and lighter. By the time it came to say evening prayers my whole demeanor changed and the transformation was truly remarkable...

I glowed like a beacon of celestial light. When folks came back that evening for prayers I greeted them all with a radiating smile and a joke... Yes, a Joke. The mood for me had turned from one of grieving to one of a rejoicing glow. I felt like singing and dancing, instead I enthusiastically sang my prayers. The people all around me started to get quite worried thinking I had flipped my lid and gone crazy. They had never accused me of being normal anyway.

At the time I could not explain my returned happiness. But, I did know my mother had not left me, she was still close-by. My love for her was as strong as ever, as it is now, at this very moment. She has gone no-where, for she is now-here inside of me. I knew I miss her physical beauty, charm and touch, but she is deep inside me and as I love her so much, I do not want her to be unhappy. I knew if I am sad, she will also be sad. Considering we are together eternally, it makes sense to make this life... a joy filled one together. My mother sends her love to you and tells me your dear heavenly Angels are watching over you.... And truly want you to enjoy your life on earth.

You should understand.... All the Mother Angels advise us that, in the final analysis, without the illusions of life and death, there would be no room for any-thing, in the physical ... to grow.

One candle can light many however its illumination cannot flame on any other candle. Likewise, our joy can light up the world but cannot shine from anyone else's mind.

SLICE THIRTY NINE
A Job Interview With God.

In a vision, you see a position advertised that everybody would love and it is to work for a great boss with infinite possibilities. It is a dream come true opportunity and whatever calling you most desired, that would be the situation you would be applying for. It brings full health benefits which means you can help to prevent the onset of disease. It supplies enough money to give security and contentment and most meaningfully, the project keeps you in Joy 24 hours a day, every day.

Wow what a job! Who wouldn't want to apply for that? So how would you go about getting your most desired employment from a boss who knows every thought in your head? What would you write down on paper as your resume? Think about it for a short while before you go any further and read my application resume.

My Dear... Celestial Director, you know every thought in my head, yet you still want me to apply for this job in writing. Since you know all my faults and strengths, I would like you to train me to reduce my faults and to increase my strengths so that I can serve in your excellent company in the best way possible.

Therefore, the best thing I can say about myself in this resume is, I will be a most enthusiastic employee in your company and will do my utmost to improve its service and products you provide to other folks. For the more we help others, the better acquainted we will become with your company and we will all grow together. You can teach me to co-create things of beauty that will enhance life on earth. In this way your company will be an intricate part of every person's life... a "window" to the materialistic world.

If we have an over-seer, who knows all there is to know about everyone, then it sure makes sense to listen to the directions that can be provided, so that everyone can prosper together ... I believe there are still a few openings available for anyone interested in joining the "Image Making Enter-prize" Who want to be in The Grand Architects Company?

Silence is the key to Gods kingdom. That is where all the creative treasures are stored and they are yours for the taking ... just so long as your intent is pure. There are no fake keys, for sometimes we find treasures, to only find them fading from our grasp, because they were taken for the wrong reason. The history books are filled with folks who gained money and power only to find a wasted, empty, miserable life. When we co-create with Gods Spirit, prosperity.... "In the Now" and "In Blissful Eternity" is assured. Congratulations, I just heard you got the job ... Enjoy your new engagement in True Spirit.

Millions have perished by man-made perceptions of be-lie-f. All the while, authentic truth awaits those who are not afraid to discover and live by it.

SLICE FORTY
Quantum Harmony.

For thousands of year's religious dogma and tribal superstitions kept scientific thinkers in a locked box. Many outspoken scholars were executed because their scientific findings were looked upon as heresy. It is only in the past two hundred years that free academic study of science was allowed to flourish unhindered by ancient religious doctrines.

Once academic scientific studies were established they rejected and ridiculed anything spiritual or metaphysical if it could not be proven by a mathematical formula. Even in today's world a few professors and scientists are closed minded to anything that resembles spirituality, but things are changing at a very rapid pace. Just as religion had to succumb to scientific knowledge, so now, science is beginning to unravel the mysteries of the universe with Quantum physics and their latest findings are stretching science into the realms of metaphysical spirituality.

After all is said and done, there can only be one truth that explains the creation/evolving of the universe, but there may be many pathways, within one truth, that will explain humanities curiosity of the cosmic puzzles.

Quantum science is going beyond the probe of atoms, photons, neutrons, quirks and exploring a newer string theory (dancing, unobservable, vibrational waves of energy) and membrane theory (Multiple universes, carved up into slices, living side by side).

Together they give room to explore what is know as the M-theory which is undertaking to prove the unity of Gravity, Electromagnetism, Weak and Strong nuclear forces. The deeper Quantum physicists explore, the closer they encircle metaphysical philosophy. They are realizing there are higher realities within infinite dimensions of intelligent vibrational energy.

Ever since humans could look up at the stars at night they have pondered the mystical magic of the cosmos. Many great ancient dynasties such as the Egyptian, Greek, Roman and Chinese debated the awe and wonder of the heavens. Brilliant, illustrious philosophers such as Plato, Aristotle, Confucius and many more, have talked about human kinds connection to the invisible eternal flows of energy that govern the Cosmos. And now, within the next hundred years, mathematical proof will uncover the connection between science, philosophy and spirituality.

It seems string theorists have uncovered eleven dimensions to our universe. Some Quantum Physicists even go so far as to state the dimensions of the universe may be infinite. At the same time they are theorizing on parallel universes that live side by side with our universe. Perhaps an infinite number of universes?

If this is proven to be true it will explain why our world was not formed by chance, for if there is an infinite number of universes, then it stands to common sense at least one would contain intelligent life as found here on earth. It can be no fluke, because of the infinite variety of universes. The formula to create our universe must differ from each and every other universe, in the same manner as no two humans are identical and each has their own free will to act within an inescapable framework.

The chances that there is another earth similar to ours in another universe are very slim indeed, for if there are two identical universes, one would be enmeshed in another, unless of course the universes are holograms of each other in different dimensions? But that would not give a variety of different universes and that seems improbable.

Even on the more basic levels medical science is engaged in many studies of spirituality within the fields of neurology, psychology many other sections of medicine. Mental illnesses that may be caused by stress and erroneous thoughts are being treated with many alternative, spiritually related treatments, which were rejected a few years ago. At every level, open minded professors, scientists and physicians are welcoming metaphysical philosophers and spiritual masters to help in the quest to eradicated disease, pollution and many other ills of human kind.

All the resources of humanity will be required to solve the mysteries of our universe and beyond. As long as all lines of communication are kept open and no learning institution will favor one subject; namely science, at the expense of neglecting metaphysics or spirituality, then the world of Quantum

Metaphysical Spiritual Science will blossom and bloom.... Humanity can at last realize they are one harmonious unit within a unified symphonic universe... Maybe that unity on earth will make Albert Einstein a very happy camper as he looks at earth from his eternal cosmic home.

If you're driving force lacks joy, your destination of accomplishments may seem meaningless, no matter how many accolades or money acc-rues.

SLICE FORTY ONE
The Lives of Metaphysical Cakes.

Humanity is constantly trying to find answers to questions that seem un-answerable. Einstein said "I want to know what God is thinking everything else is just details" Well, if we metaphysically look inside a human brain, examine how it was formed; perhaps we may get an inkling of what Einstein's non-religious God was thinking.

The universe is a united unit of evolving creation, but it needs to magnet-ize opposites, in opposing directions and have them smash into each other to shape material forms and shapes. Therefore, unity requires conflicting energies to form various forms of matter.

For simplicity, let's think about the cosmos in terms of a universal caterer who wants to cook a new delicious, delectable life force called 'cake' and everything that embodies life is a variety of cake.

Before the beginning of time, there was a void waiting to be filled. All the ingredients to bake a cake were simmering on a low light, waiting to be formed. A master baker was dreaming up a whole cook book full of recipes filled with intelligent energy. At the appropriate moment the oven was opened and there was a big bang. All the ingredients flew out of the black hole oven. It started to form elements and compounds that would eventually make a variety of cakes on a planet called earth. It infused earth with all the physical ingredients and compounds to make many different types of cake.

The universal mixture brought together over billions of years of evolving/ creating. Eventually, planet earth formed and it developed into a world filled with many cakes. In the genesis of life on earth, all types of micro-crumbs evolved into a larger material form. These microscopic bacteria would one day evolve into an excellent cake that named itself ... Homo sapiens.

As time progressed, small types of cake were fashioned into a variety of life that could move and grow through its own evolved/created intelligence system. A few mixtures later and after many millions of years of cooking, larger mammals were formed...It was at that period of time that the mix really started to heat-up and the primate cake was at last beginning to become a reality. After four billion years, human beings became a human cake on earth that contained all the 'good' wholesome ingredients the universe could supply... "All was good."

Perhaps the first human type cake was baked some two hundred thousand years ago? They only thought of themselves as just another type of cake ... Possibly they could tell they were a little different in appearance and skills. Nevertheless, they thought of themselves as a cake like all the other cakes. They shared life on earth with all the animal cakes, plants and vegetation cakes, respecting everyone's space.

The beautiful human cake contains multiple layers of intelligence. The superb part of the cake is controlled by a cake brain. It comprises of three distinct stages of evolution/creation. As far as any scientific chef can ascertain the present day cake brain contains three interconnecting parts.

Section one, is the ancient member that contains all the elements to survive dangers and climate changes. It also contains the intelligence to develop two other sections and to recognize how to evolve in-tune with earth's constant, sometimes violent, changes.

Perhaps it also has open channels to access information from outside its own fields of intelligence. Maybe it has an Ariel (invisible to science, in the same way thoughts cannot be read) that can access intelligent, vibrational energy waves, which are encouraged to travel into other compartments of the brain, to be analyzed and understood?... One part of the brain will perhaps turn the information it receives, from the central arena, into some new hi-tech material shape, or perhaps a new composition of music, poetry or art?

The human cakes intelligence was formulated from the same source of intelligent information it now receives via thought. Maybe in today's world, some human cakes don't like to be called cakes, but that maybe because they are passed their egos sell by date.

Section two, the vintage section, leant how to evolve from all the other cakes. It learnt how to stand upright and use its hands to create tools, which in turn, helped to develop and spark section three into action.

Section three, is the modern section of the brain cake at the advanced primate intelligence/intellect level. In all three sections, there lives a duality of thoughts, within a unified field of intelligence. The more developed the brain cake, the more intellectual duality thinking expands and the further removed it becomes from the original model.

The modern layer of the brain, namely the outer cortex, is overflowing with intellect that no other cake possesses on earth. It can reason and logically work things out that no other cake could ever do. It labels things and has a self-recognition that divides itself from all other cakes. It no longer calls itself a cake. It thinks it is a species named human being. Alas, no other cake in the universe knows what that means? This does not stop this cake from changing its identity and today it really believes it can control the world it inhabits.

Science understands that refined foods are depleted in goodness and nourishment, because all the natural wholesome essentials are taken out of them. Perhaps the human cake brain should not become too refined, for it may deplete all the original wisdom it was programmed to project.

It could be claimed that the modern section of the brain is the icing on the cake, considering it does contain great genius skills, but sadly, in many instances, it also believes it is the whole cake itself. Unfortunately, the good ingredients have become tainted with an opposing force that is not designed to be in the cake mix.

"You must love the crust of the earth on which you dwell more than the sweet crust of any bread or cake. You must be able to extract nutriment out of a sand-heap. You must have so good an appetite as this, else you will live in vain." _ Henry David Thoreau.

The human cake reinvented itself as a sophisticated intellect and it has taken over the whole planet and all the other perfectly formed cakes. The human cake turned into a refined human being that began to bake its own ideas. It eats and destroys too many of the other cakes. It even inflicts damage to the storeroom (earth) that supplied all its bodily, physical compounds and elements essential for survival

The outer section of the brain is designed to use the wisdom of the ancient part of the brain that has evolved through millions of years of development.

Regrettably, many times, the powerful modern outer rim of the brain bypasses the old parts and fabricates its own refined skills to be stored in the memory banks for future reference. This means it is ignoring authentic information built into the system over millions of years and is now living with beliefs, and ideas derived from thoughts, that desire control of everything it thinks it should possess.

The human brain has created its own sophisticated monsters and has allowed them to take over every section of the mind (whole person) it can consciously control. In turn, it tries to control all the other human cakes on planet earth ... (Golly Gosh! says an observant five year old child, all that will do is to turn well formed cake into crumbs!)

That is exactly what has been happening on earth for the past six thousand years (give or take a few thousand) the more advanced the human intellect/ ego becomes; the more destructive are its powers over everything it wants to control.

Humanity should be able to look towards the universities and other education systems to solve humanities problems. Regrettably, in many instances, it is the education system itself, which has become the biggest problem ... Large sections of academia shelter, in a brain-wave-set, that will-not allow itself, to be changed, by authentic meaningfulness.

It has baked its own pies-in-the-sky.... Its own man-made erroneous flavors and seasoning are being taught to students, who hunger for knowledge and leaning, ... so that they can earn lots of money to spend, on all the luxuries they have been programmed to believe will bring them happiness. Today we find a world filled with greed and fear, with no real remedy available, which will be acceptable to those who control academia. We have produced well-baked cakes with half-baked ideas, beliefs, philosophies, religions, science and knowledge.

Perhaps academia would do well to remember an old saying from Zen legend/sage Bodhidharma....

"If you use your mind to study reality, you won't understand either your mind or reality. If you study reality without using your mind, you'll understand both. People capable of true vision, know that the mind is empty."

That passage was written around fifteen hundred years ago ... Maybe the scribes meaning was; To balance the mind, we have to go into the ancient center, and within the center, in the silence of a pool of wisdom, true thoughts can be located, that will give humanity all the information it requires, to live an authentic life on earth.

Maybe, at the center of the human mind is a doorway or wormhole that takes the mind to an infinite source of wisdom?

Maybe that is where all the great discoveries and creativity of the past and present derives its information?

Maybe that is where all authentic people find the wisdom to live objectively detached from all the anxiety and worry the modern world fabricates.

Maybe humanity can progress with all three sections of the brain working in unity within its whole mind and all other minds on earth.

Will humanity locate the authentic recipes that were baked into its intuitive brain, when the master chief was creating the metaphysical ingredients that make up an authentic, soulful human being?

Alternatively, will the human race continue to refine itself into sophistic intellectual extinction? Why I do believe, it is time for afternoon tea... Divine celestial carrot cake, with heavenly, soulful preserves. Now that what I call a wonder-ful belief.

Home is where the heart is ... Its love & joy will point the way forward.

SLICE FORTY TWO
Will Clones Have Souls?

The Spiritual Future of Artificial Intelligence

There is much controversy today over the cloning of human beings. Scientists have successfully cloned sheep and other animals and it can only be a matter of time before we have walking, talking replicas of ourselves. I am not getting into the discussion of whether it is wrong or right, for that will be a debate that will rage for a long time to come. Science and religion have always been at loggerheads with each other. There is no wrong or right and many wars are caused by strong beliefs that rely on the ego's view of the world. The only truth is spirit's truth, not just the stand-alone human ego.

The Question here is will a clone have a soul? I asked this question recently on a spiritual forum and the views of some very well respected spiritual folks were quite mixed. I concluded that it all depends on how we define a soul and who we think we are. These are deep probing questions and many philosophers of the past have come up with a variety of answers, but humanity as a whole has not settled on any one answer to date. So what is the answer? Let's look into the future and take one scenario:

A person by the name of Will is fifty years old and lives as an atheist. Will has undergone many cosmetic surgeries for vanity. Does Will have a soul? Of course he does; right? He may not recognize God, but that does not mean God does not exist. Atheists may not know if they have a soul, which does not mean they do not have one.

Now Will is very wealthy and decides he would like a clone of himself so his image is left behind after he dies. The clone is made and is physically identical to how Will looked when he was young - all natural with no cosmetic surgery. The clone studies hard, grows up very religious and becomes a priest. Does the minister not have a soul? Will God disown the minister?

Who is to cast the first stone? Is the "Will" of God the same as the "Will" of the clone?

What about the advancement with microchips? Very soon we will have robots that can think for themselves. Maybe solar powered, or they may even be powered by inhaling oxygen. Science fiction is fast becoming science reality. Androids may well look just like humans, but that is artificial life and a machine will not have a soul — or will it? Maybe artificial humans will be able to manufacture "real" flesh and blood humans who are genetically altered never to develop a sickness or harbor infectious germs It may well be the machines become more intelligent than humans and we are ruled by them. Extreme thoughts maybe, but everything than now seems improbable, is remarkably possible sometime in the future.

Now more than ever folks need to understand who they are and the reason they exist. If we go through life with no idea of who we truly are, we will get more and more lost in the high-tech revolution. We need a sound foundation to build our lives upon.Every life-form contains a soul, and even a clone will have a soul once the breath of life is infused into the body. We will never be able to know who was born and who is a clone. Spirit is in all life and those that want to think humans have an exclusive contract with spirit will feel anger and hatred towards a cloned human, if they can distinguish one from a naturally created human. Many folks will say a clone has no soul therefore is not really human.

Many folks think they are superior to a dog or cat. Many folks believe animals don't possess a soul. All this blind "dogma" has been programmed in humans for thousands of years. That is why most folks can't be happy. They have to guard their possessions and many humans believe that they possess God exclusively, from all other species of life. Some fanatical fundamentalists even go so far as to think other humans, who are not of their belief system, are not in God's camp at all. Many different tribes entangled in limitations of thought, lined up in divisions of ego's blind thinking and so much time wasted, worrying and hating others.

Oh! by the way, did I mention genetic engineering? I think I did mention it and said it was a possibility in the future. Well, I heard today they can put genes in our foods to make us fit and well. Maybe also to control our minds, just in case we feel like rioting against the clones? Athletes are experimenting with all kinds of stuff to make them compete faster. One-hundredth of a second can mean the difference of big money sponsorship, and athletes will try anything to make themselves winners. The latest thing I read was wasp juice from the larvae of killer hornets gives a big boost. Some seek a menu of caterpillar fungus, seal penis and extract of sea horse. How lip-smackingly scrumptious!

With such competition in sports, it will not be long before gene therapy is introduced and injected into sports folk. We will be able to tailor-make our bodies. New stem cells of old diseased cells... No need of the surgeon's scalpel. So we will re-manufacture a human being to suit a trend. We will become designer beings. Stem cells are cloned cells so many humans will be injected with cloned cells. Does this mean they will lose their soul? Does it mean they may be able to clone a soul? The possibilities of modern science boggles the mind. The cures for many diseases maybe just a few years away? No illness means longer lives. Can the planet cope with a population explosion?

This is just a brief glimpse into the future. What would folks say who lived two hundred years ago and could comment on today's lifestyles? Whatever will be will be. Science will advance and humans will survive in spite of their ego selves. The moments of life are precious and few. We are put on earth to enjoy our lives and what wonderment there is to see a sunrise, to hear the birds sing, to gaze at a sunset. The free things in life are enough. Simplicity in all things is the answer in any era. Everything else is just the icing on the cake. How big a slice do we need?

Remember: Enjoy life and don't fret about so-called advancements. All is perfection in the soul's world and that is the real eternal world. We are all souls together and nothing can alter spirit. We all need to recognize we are the energy that drives the motor, we are not the motor. We are the energy that feeds the mind, we are not the mind. We are the energy that feeds the thoughts, we are not the thoughts. We take a ride on the carousel of life, but we must remember not to go round so fast or it will make us sick and dizzy. The seesaw makes for one down and one up and we don't want others down at our expense. So let's get of the seesaw chaos of living as segment societies...

Let's become the best we can be ... Best we all ascend in spirits' optimum elevator together and live life with a higher view of each other.

Depressions are like a bad game of golf and sooner or later expire... Just remember to keep your head up and smile when people moan and swing through the negativity.

SLICE FORTY THREE
A Real Cool Reality.

We have all been told sometime in our lives to "Get Real Dude", but what does this mean? Just what is our reality and how can we change our perception of what we have been taught to believe as reality? If a wasp stings us it hurts. If we buy a stock or bond and it halves in value we "feel" the sting in a different manner. This sure feels real enough. Just simple things like having a contractor make repairs to our home can devastate some of us. We have all been told by a workman "Don't Worry, I will treat your home as though it is my own." Little did we know the guy lives in Pompeii!

Throughout our live many events will come along to test our resolve. Some of these events are happy, some are sad. As long as we draw breath there will be a continuation of daily actions which we will make us react. Some of these we have a certain amount of control over. Some we have none. These events are part and parcel of the human experience and whilst we may not like all that goes on, the show will go on all the same.

We look around and our eyes show us a scene of our surroundings but everything is constantly changing so how real can that be. When we look towards the sky we see the stars but many of them no longer exist. They disappeared billions of years ago but we still see their light.

The light we receive comes from the Sun. All the magnificent colors we see all around are gasses burning on the Sun. They are filtered through the light that hits earth and react to various particles of matter. So you could say color is an illusion. We just see the millions of different shades and marvel at the beauty. The reality is in the invisible rays of light. In Physics color is described as a theoretical property that distinguishes the various states in which quarks exist. In other words matter mirrors anti matter.

You are reading this article and the very second you digest the information it has become history. Each moment becomes the past in an instant. We live our lives as a grain of sand trickling through an hour glass. An hour, a day, a month, a century, all pass in a fleeting flash. We can make plans for the future but what if we are not around to fulfill our dreams. What we must understand is nothing stays the same. Nothing is that serious that it takes away the Joy of the moment.

Every cell, molecule and atom in our bodies will all change over a two year period. So even our physical being is different from what it was. If we only see life through a limited perspective of what we know, then it can be compared to being invited to an amazing banquet and only eating bread and water.

I have recently returned from a two week tour of Italy and have visited many Churches, Basilicas, Temples and Holy Shrines. All the monuments depict the cultures and religions spanning two thousand years. Throughout this period of magnificent building, wars, suffering, bigotry and hatred was being perpetrated by the very folks who were giving orders to build the holy shrines. Following our Egos limited perspective of life has lead to many disastrous actions. A total misunderstanding of reality and we base our culture on similar rules and regulations today.

We have learnt nothing from two thousand years of mayhem. At this very moment many wars are going on in the world today. Tribes still defend or attack via their versions of erroneous realities. People are still living in suppressed and poor conditions in third world countries and even in the rich countries, people suffer mentally. What is it all about? Why do we continue to adopt a lifestyle that is harmful mentally and then manifesting into physical sickness?

We must come to terms with our perception of reality. If things are constantly changing and nothing stays the same, what is there to worry about? Nothing can be considered as real for nothing physical lasts. NO MATTER WHAT, NO MATTER LASTS.

As we detach our memories from the shackles of the past we begin find peace of mind. We Release the conditioned minds narrow view of how we would like life to be. We are now attaching our thoughts to a power source that is everlasting and will not fail us. No short circuit.

No disappointment.

No illusion.

No worry.

No anxiety.

All the real things that enhance our lives cannot be seen, touched and felt in the physical way. They will be transported into our senses so that we will see, hear, feel, touch and smell The Divine and this will come to us when we are in a sense of Joy. There is the yardstick of our attachment. Beyond wants... Beyond needs...Beyond the physical traumas of everyday life.

Just as our shadow is a reflection of our physical form, just as a mirror is a reflection of our form, our physical form is a reflection of our true selves. Billions of invisible particles are floating around to form different life forms. The blueprint of a human gene is a copy of invisible matter, which is our true identity.

In the silence of our thoughtless mind our soul will connect us to our reality and once we feel the Eternal Infinite Touch of God we will not want to go back to living a false reality. We will transform into a Healthy Wealth Wise Powerhouse of Joy for all our friends and family to follow.

There will always be those who will ridicule and belittle us, but I think we will be able to handle that, don't you. There is an old saying which goes "TRY" and if at first you don't succeed "TRY" "TRY" AGAIN. We will find there is no effort involved in finding happiness enshrined in love. There was never any effort and no need "To TRY" for there is no failure. It is all a learning experience and the longer we live the more we learn. We will continue to find our true selves and become one with all that is REAL. We will learn to trust our instincts more.

We will find our awareness of dangers is stronger, so we will avoid trouble. We will become more tolerant of other and learn to forgive passed hurtful experiences.

The need to defend will be replaced with the need to love. We are transient beings living in a finite form. We live on the tick of a clock, moments in time, and then the moment is gone. There are billions of invisible particles that are our true being. We are constructed from our own reality and possess infinite possibility for we born out of eternity.

We are given freedom of choice within a whole range of possibilities, preprogrammed, yet free willed at the same time. Our thought dimensions are our image creators, which filter through our imagination. As we unlock our treasures of the Cosmos, we will begin to understand the meaning of real. Spirit colors our thoughts with the paintbrush of the Soul.

As we sail through life we will slowly uncover our true self and the joy of each experience becomes more and more ecstatic. A flotilla of magical moment, journeying to a mystical paradise. We release the memories of fear and our emotions are ablaze with the Joy of knowing we are connected to all that exists, Dimensions of the Real flood our brain cells.

When the time comes to live in the "real" totally, we will be back home in Eternity. For now our reality is to enjoy each moment and that is A Real Cool Reality.

God wears a real colorful designer Label.

*When we live with **GOD** (Grand-pa/ma Opens Doors) we be-long...When we live with **EGO** (Ease God Out) we be-short.*

SLICE FORTY FOUR
Three Days in Paradise

Imagine you were given a free holiday for three months on a paradise luxury cruise ship sailing around the world. Then you receive notice that the holiday has been cut short to just three days.

You may at first feel pangs of disappointment, but for sure, you will make the most of every second you are on your luxury voyage.

Human beings do not live forever. If a person lives beyond the age of eighty they have done better than most.

The earth has been around for well over four billion years, which we can relate to a three month cruise... Therefore, eighty years is not even as long as a three day holiday, as a percentage, in the existence of life on earth.

With such a small time frame available to each human being, how many make the most of each given moment? Well, it is never too late to make sure you are going to enjoy your holiday on earth's playground, filled with an abundant inventory of nature's treasures

Your passport was your birth and you have been lucky enough to be chosen to enjoy your three day vacation.

Day one was your birth-day.

Day two is your existence now.

Day three is your demise-day (after which you will have plenty time to reminisce in the vacuum of nothingness)

Make sure you do everything possible to savor each delectable, enchantment of the present moment.

It is not you street address that measures your worth, it is how you address your mind that will deliver the treasures of the universe.

SLICE FORTY FIVE
Dreams, Reality, the Senses and Beyond.

We are having a dream and in this dream we are in a big city that has ten lanes of fast traffic continually going through it. We are standing on the curb and wish to cross the road to get water and food, because on our side of the street there is no nourishment and if we do not get across the road we will perish. But the road has bumper to bumper trucks and vans filled with worry and anxiety, all traveling at one hundred miles an hour...How do we cross the road? There are no bridges to walk over the traffic and no subways to walk under traffic...How can we get across the road and nourish ourselves, for if we stay where we are, we will soon expire.

I did say that we are having a dream; therefore we can simply walk across the road and through all the trucks filled with a cargo of emotional garbage. We can even fly over the road once we know how to sprout wings. In dreams all things are possible and no real harm can befall us.

But what about our day time activities... Are they any different to our dreams? Who is the one experiencing each action that is performed? Many people believe the five senses of sight, hearing, taste, touch and smell are just physical experiences, but what if the senses have a life force of their own. What if the senses can see, hear, feel, touch and smell our true essence and they are all observing the real energy force that drives our motor (mind & body).

Our conscious mind is aware of all the senses and uses them from moment to moment, but I do not know many people who are aware their senses have a life force (dimension) of their own both local and non local and are indeed a part of our eternal self...Our Soul. For in reality our true self(Soul) is multifaceted and everything we experience through our conscious mind has a mirror image in the non physical manner, so you might well say we are observing ourselves whilst we are observing everything else we come in contact with.

I see the flower but does the flower have a vision of me?

I hear the leaves on the trees but can the leaves hear my vibrations?

I taste water but can the atoms in the water have an awareness of being in my body?

I smell a lilac plant but can the essence of the smell experience it is being savored?

I feel the texture of a blade of grass still attached to the earth, is that blade of grass aware it is being felt?

This may seem a strange way to think, but if we cannot grasp who we are, we will never live as an authentic, natural human being. We will not be aware we are living on a natural planet, filled with many intelligent energy forces that have no need of an intellect, or personal physical identity. Each essence knows it exists and that knowingness is good enough.

All life forces are made up from molecule and atoms... protons and neutrons...Sub atomic particle etc. In scientific terms life can be broken down into ten various stages of change. Without going into quantum physics, which I only have a smattering of acceptable knowledge, all changes are fed by intelligent energies. Some are known and identified as gravity and magnetic wave bands. Many force fields have yet to be discovered by name...but they are here, all around us this very moment and we can experience many unlabeled dimensions of mystical energy.

Remember I started this essay by saying we are having a dream and in any dream we can fly or do whatever we desire. Well, if we begin to understand nothing is how it seems to be and anything is possible in our minds vision of reality. Once we allow our intuition imaginativeness freedom to explore the realms of the subconscious mind that controls all our bodily function. We will discover our heart can and does use all our senses as does every cell in our body and the senses can also mirror themselves. All intelligence has a receiver and transmitter. It matters not if it is visible or invisible ... The senses are of significance to everything in the seen and unseen and live with the truth way beyond the intellectual minds experience.

To become a candle in the wind a person needs to understand they are an eternal flame.

SLICE FORTY SIX
Child's Play.

We all know children like to play imaginary games. Boys will play games such as star wars or action man (that has become too real) Girls will play with their dolls and make up lots of imaginary friends to supervise (rehearsing to be a wife and mother?) Using our imagination in role playing games is a very important stage in every child's lives.

As we grow out of childhood (this happens far too quickly these days) our imagination turns into what we consider to be reality roles. We actually become mothers and wives. We realistically become scientists doctors, salesmen etc. The role become our identities and with them comes great anxiety and stress because we need to project ourselves as what society deems to be success.

As time progresses we have found ourselves locked in a religion (or Atheism) Locked in a job identity... Locked in a family image... And locked into many habits of eating and thinking that 'Plays" havoc with our immune system and good health... So, we have stopped using our imagination and now we play a game of havoc, anticipating how long it will take us to die of a self inflicted dis-ease.

Giving the intellect/ego free run of our minds locks out all the child's play that brought us such joy as children....We have grown up and take life as a very serious justification for our realities.

We look at our bodies an find pictures of other human nude bodies... Dirty!

We find sex a dirty subject unless it is confide to marriage.

We seek out all types of foods that will destroy the cells in our bodies and ridicule and reject foods that our cells desire.

We search for quick fix remedies like alcohol, cigarettes, drugs etc to help use continue our "realistic" roles.

We meet in social groups and find comfort comradely in drinking alcohol together so that everyone pickles their brains and livers together.

Who gave us the right to overwhelm our minds & bodies?

We are only the caretakers, not the masters.

We only have the right to wreck.... what we created and we certainly did not master-mind our bodies. We did create our role plays and we do a fantastic job of demolishing our authentic child like image. We are left with other peoples handed down inept thoughts that have manufactured our conceptual, but oh! so destructive self perception.

Understand all the roles we play out every day are only make-believes.

The truth exists way beyond the role play. And if it is not the truth we live...why allow such an imaginary existence to make us sick?

The route to freedom rests not in the quest for intellectual knowledge; rather, the wisdom of a simple mind holds the keys of liberation

SLICE FORTY SEVEN
Living As the Spark.

Many times we hear about being "the divine spark" but what does this mean? We also hear people saying we need to "think positive" but if things are not going well how can we think positive? Let's use a car battery as an image of human existence. The battery is the human being and has a negative and positive side. It is of no use living in the negative and likewise it is no use living as a positive, for there is no connection to any energy. They are both "dead" entities on their own that have no life. But what happens when they are connected to a central point? Miraculously they Spark. We have made a connection and we have found a live energy.

Now what if we could live as the spark and then go the positive connection and live a life of joy filled energy? Does this make sense...To live as the electrical spark and feed the energy into a positive life. That is a big difference than living as a positive thinking person looking for a spark.

There is no doubt that all materialize substances contain a positive and negative energy field but when they are separated nothing can be formed, although the spark is present all the time. It cannot be fired until two points agree to connect and become charged as one, in a powerful force of true universal energy.

You can bend it and twist it ...You can misuse and abuse it...But even God cannot change ... The Truth.

SLICE FORTY EIGHT
As High As A Kite.

I was sitting on the beach the other day watching a kite (In the shape of a two winged aircraft) flying high in the sky. It made wonderful acrobatic maneuvers as if piloted by a person with a lifetime's experience of flying. However, we all know a kite cannot fly without the power of the wind. So how real was the performance I was watching?

Firstly, it took a person with great imagination to design a kite shaped like a tiger moth aircraft that can encompass the aerodynamics to be powered by the wind. That accomplishment in itself takes great skill and awareness of the forces of nature.

Secondly, the person who purchased the kite needs to read the instructions and learn how to apply the winds forces to achieve a great display. The mind and hand coordination requires a mastery to attain the required skills.

Thirdly, without the power of the wind, the kite would just be a charming, colorful, textured replica of a Tiger Moth aircraft. We cannot see the wind....but we know it must exist, for we can feel it and see the consequences of its power.

So, we have a relationship between the designer and manufacturer which ultimately will connect to the user. It then needs a power of nature that cannot be seen in order to allow the kite to operate. The display I was observing had a lot of *behind the scenes work* that needed to be performed, before the show could go on.

But, where did the designer get his ideas from?

How did the user coordinate his thoughts with his hands?

What are the invisible forces in our lives that project all the physical actions we see all around us

And what is more important...How real are they?

Are the intangible force the true reality and are the physical things we see, taste, feel, smell and hear just a manifestation of a display that looks great, but is only a finite illusion?

Are we all flying our kites in a wind of fantasy?

Are we living a life with self- images that mask the truth of the real power of whom and what we are?

Are we living on the breezes of discontent that takes away the true Love & Joy that we are intended to live?

Somewhere beyond our brains belief system and conscious awareness, lives the cosmic truth of a reality that creates "all things." Hidden in each cell of our being exists the secrets to divine immortality that transcends humanities divisions.

The next time you observe a kite flying high in the sky, become aware of the divine cosmic power of spirit that is flying your kite (Mind) to higher, elevated levels of True Love & Authentic Joy.

Now say out loud; **"I Have The Spirit to be Wealthy, The Soul To Be Healthy And The Heart To Be Wise."**

Intellect and Intelligence may be close stable mates but one is a Hacker the other a Thoroughbred.

Slice Forty Nine
The Joys of Being a Nobody

There is a lot to be said for being inconspicuous. For one thing, no one is going to compete with your position in life. You are safe and secure being a nobody. You have complete freedom to roam where the breezes take you and never be bothered by people wanting your autograph or a lock of your hair. And just think for one moment, if you were really famous they may erect a statue of you in the town square... Then you would become a target for every bird to poop on your head. Yes indeed, when you can declare you are a nobody you have triumphed over the best of the best. And speaking of the best - God is also a No-Body - so you are in celebrated company.

The Man From Nowhere

The mask slips as the doors close,
Time to undertake an invisible Pose
A man from nowhere, who nobody knows,
Obscure and aloof, from societies shows.

The nameless one, no symbol or label,
All the cards lay bare, on the banquet table,
Blowing in the wind, that once rocked his cradle,
A prince among men, now only a fable.

A statue standing in the town square,
People gather, to gaze and stare,
They look for a second, but really don't care,
Alas, the lonely figure, of the man from nowhere.

An icon to the world, now fertile as the land,
Quietly drifts through time, a solitary grain of sand,

Echo wisps of voice, eerie ghostly command,
The man from nowhere, no longer in-demand.

Once we can let go of a problem the solution will seek us out.

Final Poetic Thought

On Tour

Inside the petals of joyful exploration, a souls journey ventures to un-known abodes, the beating heart's rhythmic drums send messages towards an open mind, dancing with virtue n grace, a baby is born ... everything is in divine order, now heart - mind - soul are as one, at peace, in harmony with all of mother nature, the tour of a lifetime is about to emerge on earths sa-cred playground, God given de-lights, for all who are aware of the mystical maestro presents.

Michael Levy is the author of ten Inspirational books. For more information go to his website: http://www.pointoflife.com

www.ingramcontent.com/pod-product-compliance
Lightning Source LLC
Chambersburg PA
CBHW060818120626
46557CB00001B/260